ON A SIDE-TRACK

and

A TOUCH OF SUN

ON A SIDE-TRACK
and
A TOUCH OF SUN

Mary Hallock Foote

PP

Portmay Press
New York

"On a Side-Track" was originally published in 1895 as part of the collection *The Cup of Trembling*; "A Touch of Sun" was originally published in 1903 in a collection by the same name. Both stories are now part of the public domain.

Cover image: *Winter Landscape,* Pekka Halonen, 1926

Published in 2024 by Portmay Press, New York

ISBN 978-1-959986-26-3 (paperback)
ISBN 978-1-959986-27-0 (ebook)

PP

Portmay Press
244 Madison Avenue
New York, NY 10016
www.portmaypress.com

ON A SIDE-TRACK

I

It was the second week in February, but winter had taken a fresh hold: the stockmen were grumbling; freight was dull, and travel light on the white Northwestern lines. In the Portland car from Omaha there were but four passengers: father and daughter—a gentle, unsophisticated pair—and two strong-faced men, fellow-travelers also, keeping each other's company in a silent but close and conspicuous proximity. They shared the same section, the younger man sleeping above, going to bed before, and rising later than, his companion; and whenever he changed his seat or made an unexpected movement, the eyes of the elder man followed him, and they were never far from him at any time.

The elder was a plain farmer type of man, with a clean-shaven, straight upper lip, a grizzled beard covering the lower half of his face, and humorous wrinkles spreading from the corners of his keen gray eyes.

The younger showed in his striking person that union of good blood with hard conditions so often seen in the old-young graduates of the life schools of the West. His hands and face were dark with exposure to the sun, not of parks and club-grounds and seaside piazzas, but the dry untempered light of the desert and the plains. His dark eye was distinctively masculine—if there be such a thing as gender in features—bold, ardent, and possessive; but now it was clouded with sadness that did not pass like a mood, though he looked capable of moods.

He was dressed in the demi-toilet which answers for dinners in the West, on occasions where a dress-coat is not required. In itself the costume was correct, even fastidious, in its details, but on board an overland train there was a foppish unsuitability in it that "gave the wearer away," as another man would have said—put him at a disadvantage, notwithstanding his splendid physique, and the sad, rather fine preoccupation of his manner. He looked like a very real person dressed for a trifling part, which he lays aside between the scenes while he thinks about his sick child, or his debts, or his friend with whom he has quarreled.

But these incongruities, especially the one of dress, might easily have escaped a pair of eyes so confiding and unworldly as those of the young girl in the opposite section; they had escaped her, but not the incongruity of youth with so much sadness. The girl and her father had boarded the car at Omaha, escorted by the porter of one of the forward sleepers on the same train. They had come from farther East. The old gentleman appeared to be an invalid; but they gave little trouble. The porter had much leisure on his hands, which he bestowed in arrears of sleep on the end seat forward. The conductor made up his accounts in the empty drawing-room, or looked at himself in the mirrors, or stretched his legs on the velvet sofas. He was a young fellow, with a tendency to jokes and snatches of song and talk of a light character when not on duty. He talked sometimes with the porter in low tones, and then both looked at the pair of travelers in No. 8, and the younger man seemed moodily aware of their observation.

On the first morning out from Omaha the old gentleman kept his berth until nine or ten o'clock. At eight his daughter brought him a cup of chocolate and a sandwich, and sat between his curtains, chatting with him cozily. In speaking together they used the language of the Society of Friends.

The young man opposite listened attentively to the girl's voice; it was as sweet as the piping of birds at daybreak. Phebe her father called her.

Afterward Phebe sat in the empty section next her father's. The table before her was spread with a fresh napkin, and a few pieces of old household silver and china which she had taken from her lunch-basket.

She and her father were economical travelers, but in all their belongings there was the refinement of modest suitability and an exquisite cleanliness. Her own order for breakfast was confined to a cup of coffee, which the porter was preparing in the buffet-kitchen.

"Would you mind changing places with me?"

The young man in No. 8 spoke to his companion, who sat opposite reading a newspaper. They changed seats, and by this arrangement the younger could look at Phebe, who innocently gave him every advantage to study her sober and delicate profile against the white snow-light, as she sat watching the dreary cattle-ranges of Wyoming swim past the car window.

Her hair had been brushed, and her face washed in the bitter alkaline waters of the plains, with the uncompromising severity of one whose standards of personal adornment are limited to the sternest ideals of neatness and purity. Yet her fair face bloomed, like a winter sunrise, with tints of rose and pearl and sapphire blue, and the pale gold of winter sunshine was in her satin-smooth hair.

The young man did not fail to include in his study of Phebe the modest breakfast equipment set out before her. He perfectly recalled the pattern of the white-and-gold china, the touch, the very taste, of the thin, bright old silver spoons; they were like his grandmother's tea-things in the family homestead in the country, where he had spent his summers as a boy. The look of them touched him nearly, but not happily, it would seem, from his expression.

The porter came with the cup of coffee, and offered a number of patronizing suggestions in the line of his service, which the young girl declined. She set forth a meek choice of food, blushing faintly in deprecation of the young man's eyes, of which she began to be aware. Evidently she was not yet hardened to the practice of eating in public.

He took the hint, and retired to his corner, opening a newspaper between himself and Phebe.

Presently he heard her call the porter in a small, ineffectual voice. The porter did not come. She waited a little, and called again, with no better result. He put down his newspaper.

"If you will press the button at your left," he suggested.

"The button!" she repeated, looking at him helplessly.

He sprang to assist her. As he did so his companion flung down his paper, and jumped in front of him. The eyes of the two met. A hot flush rose to the young man's eyebrows.

"I am calling the porter for her."

"Oh!" said the other, and he sat down again; but he kept an eye upon the angry youth, who leaned across Phebe's seat, and touched the electric button.

"Little girl hadn't got on to it, eh?" the grizzled man remarked pleasantly, when his companion had resumed his seat.

There was no answer.

"Nice folks; from the country, somewheres back East, I should guess," the imperturbable one continued. "Old man seems sort of sickly. Making a move on account of his health, likely. Great mistake—old folks turning out in winter huntin' a climate."

The young man remained silent, and the elder returned to his paper.

At Cheyenne, where the train halts for dinner, the young girl helped her father into his outer garments, buttoned herself hastily into her homespun jacket bordered with gray fur, pinned her little hat firmly to her crown of golden braids, hid her hands in her muff—she did not wait to put on gloves—and led the way to the dining-room.

The travelers in No. 8 disposed of their meal rapidly, in their usual close but silent conjunction, and returned at once to the car.

The old gentleman and his daughter walked the windy platform, and cast rather forlorn glances at the crowd bustling about in the bleak winter sunlight. When they took their seats again, the father's pale blue eyes were still paler, his face looked white and drawn with the cold; but Phebe was like a rose: with her wonderful, pure color the girl was beautiful. The young man of No. 8 looked at her with a startled reluctance, as if her sweetness wounded him.

Then he seemed to have resolved to look at her no more. He leaned his head back in his corner, and closed his eyes; the train shook him slightly as he sat in moody preoccupation with his thoughts, and the miles of track flew by.

At Green River, at midnight, the Portland car was dropped by its convoy of the Union Pacific, and was coupled with a train making up for the Oregon Short Line. There was hooting and backing of engines, slamming of car doors, flashing of conductors' lanterns, voices calling across the tracks. One of these voices could be heard, in the wakeful silence within the car, as an engine from the west steamed past in the glare of its snow-wreathed headlight.

"No. 10 stuck this side of Squaw Creek. Bet you don't make it before Sunday!"

The outbound conductor's retort was lost in the clank of couplings as the train lurched forward on the slippery rails.

"Phebe, is thee awake?" the old gentleman softly called to his daughter, about the small hours.

"Yes, father. Want anything?"

"Are those ventilators shut? I feel a cold draft in the back of my berth."

The ventilators were all shut, but the train was now climbing the Wind River divide, the cold bitterly increasing, and the wind dead ahead. Cinders tinkled on the roaring stovepipes, the blast swept the car roofs, pelting the window panes with fine, dry snow, and searching every joint and crevice defended by the company's upholstery.

Phebe slipped down behind the berth-curtain, and tucked a shawl in at her father's back. Her low voice could be heard, and the old man's self-pitying tones in answer to her tender questionings. He coughed at intervals till daybreak, when there was silence in section No. 7.

In No. 8, across the aisle, the young man lay awake in the strength of his thoughts, and made up passionate sentences which he fancied himself speaking to persons he might never be brought face to face with again. They were people mixed in with his life in various relations, past and present, whose opinions had weighed with him. When he heard Phebe talking to her father, he muttered, with a sort of anguish:

"Oh, you precious lamb!"

He and his companion made their toilet early, and breakfasted and smoked together, and their taciturn relation continued as before. Snow filled the air, and blotted out the distance, but there were few stationary dark objects outside by which to gauge its fall. They were across the border now, between Wyoming and Idaho, in a featureless white region, a country of small Mormon ranches, far from any considerable town.

The old man slept behind his curtains. Phebe went through the morning routine by which women travelers make themselves at home and pass the time, but obviously her day did not begin until her father had reported himself. She had found a hole in one of her gloves, which she was mending, choosing critically the needle and the silk for the purpose from a very complete housewife in brown linen bound with a brown silk galloon. Again the young man was reminded of his boyhood, and of certain kind old ladies of precise habits who had contributed to his happiness, and occasionally had eked out the fond measure of paternal discipline.

The snow continued; about noon the train halted at a small water station, waited awhile as if in consideration of difficulties ahead, and then quietly backed down upon a side-track. A shock of silence followed. Every least personal movement in the thinly peopled car, before lost in the drumming of the wheels, asserted itself against this new medium. The passengers looked up and at one another; the Pullman conductor stepped out to make inquiries.

The silence continued, and became embarrassing. Phebe dropped her scissors. This time the young man sat still, but the flush rose to his forehead as before. The old gentleman's breathing could be heard behind his curtains; the porter rattling plates in the cooking-closet; the soft rustling of the snow outside. Phebe stepped to her father's berth, and peeped between his curtains; he was still sleeping. Her voice was hushed to the note of a sick-room as she asked—

"Where are we now, do you know?"

The young man was looking at her, and to him she addressed the question.

With a glance at his companion, he crossed to her side of the car, and took the seat in front of her.

"We are in the Bear Lake valley, just over the border of Idaho, about fifteen miles from the Squaw Creek divide," he answered, sinking his voice.

"Did you hear what that person said in the night, when a train passed us, about our not getting through?"

"I wondered if you heard that." He smiled. "You did not rest well, I'm afraid."

"I was anxious about father. This weather is a great surprise to us. We were told the winters were short in southern Idaho—almost like Virginia; but look at this!"

"We have nearly eight thousand feet of altitude here, you must remember. In the valleys it is warmer. There the winter does break usually about this time. Are you going on much farther?"

"To a place called Volney."

"Volney is pretty high; but there is Boise, farther down. Strangers moving into a new country very seldom strike it right the first time."

"Oh, we shall stay at Volney, even if we do not like it; that is, if we *can* stay. I have a married sister living there. She thought the climate would be better for father."

After a pause she asked, "Do you know why we are stopping here so long?"

"Probably because we have had orders not to go any farther."

"Do you mean that we are blocked?"

"The train ahead of us is. We shall stay here until that gets through."

"You seem very cheerful about it," she said, observing his expression.

"Ah, I should think so!"

His short lip curled in the first smile she had seen upon his strong, brooding face. She could not help smiling in response, but she felt bound to protest against his irresponsible view of the situation.

"Have you so much time to spend upon the road? I thought the men of this country were always in a hurry."

"It makes a difference where a man is going, and on what errand, and what fortune he meets with on the way. *I* am not going to Volney."

She did not understand his emphasis, nor the bearing of his words. His eyes dropped to her hands lying in her lap, still holding the glove she had been mending.

"How nicely you do it! How can you take such little stitches without pricking yourself, when the train is going?"

"It is my business to take little stitches. I don't know how to do anything else."

"Do you mean it literally? It is your business to sew?"

The notion seemed to surprise him.

"No; I mean in a general sense. Some of us can do only small things, a stitch at a time—take little steps, and not know always where they are going."

"Is this a little step—to Volney?"

"Oh, no; it is a very long one, and rather a wild one, I'm afraid. I suppose everybody does a wild thing once in a lifetime?"

"How should you know that?"

"I only said so. I don't say that it is true."

"People who take little steps are sometimes picked up and carried off their feet by those who take long, wild ones."

"Why, what are we talking about?" she asked herself, in surprise.

"About going to Volney, was it not?" he suggested.

"What is there about Volney, please tell me, that you harp upon the name? I am a stranger, you know; I don't know the country allusions. Is there anything peculiar about Volney?"

"She is a deep little innocent," he said within himself; "but oh, so innocent!" And again he appeared to gather himself in pained resistance to some thought that jarred with the thought of Phebe. He rose and bowed, and so took leave of her, and settled himself back into his corner, shading his eyes with his hand.

He ate no luncheon, Phebe noticed, and he sat so long in a dogged silence that she began to cast wistful glances across the aisle, wondering if he were ill, or if she had unwittingly been rude to him. Any one could have shaken her confidence in her own behavior; moreover, she reminded herself, she did not know the etiquette of an overland train. She had heard that the Western people were very friendly; no doubt they expected a frank response in others. She resolved to be more careful the next time, if the moody young man should speak to her again.

Her father was awake now, dressed and sitting up. He was very chipper, but Phebe knew that his color was not natural, nor his breathing right. He was much inclined to talk, in a rambling, childish, excited manner that increased her anxiety.

The young man in No. 8 had evidently taken his fancy; his

formal, old-fashioned advances were modestly but promptly met.

"I suppose it is not usual, in these parts, for travelers to inquire each other's names?" the old gentleman remarked to his new acquaintance; "but we seem to have plenty of time on our hands; we might as well improve it socially. My name is David Underhill, and this is my daughter Phebe. Now what might thy name be, friend?"

"My name is Ludovic," said the youth, looking a half-apology at Phebe, who saw no reason for it.

"First or family name?"

"Ludovic is my family name."

"And a very good name it is," said the old gentleman. "Not a common name in these parts, I should say, but one very well and highly known to me," he added, with pleased emphasis. "Phebe, thee remembers a visit we had from Martin Ludovic when we were living at New Rochelle?"

"Thee knows I was not born when you lived at New Rochelle, father dear."

"True, true! It was thy mother I was thinking of. She had a great esteem for Martin Ludovic. He was one of the world's people, as we say—in the world, but not of the world. Yet he made a great success in life. He was her father's junior partner—rose from a clerk's stool in his counting-room; and a great success he made of it. But that was after Friend Lawrence's time. My wife was Phebe Lawrence."

Young Ludovic smiled brightly in reply to this information, and seemed about to speak, but the old gentleman forestalled him.

"Friend Lawrence had made what was considered a competence in those days—a very small one it would be called now; but he was satisfied. Thee may not be aware that it is a recommendation among the Friends, and it used to be a common practice, that when a merchant had made a sufficiency for himself and those depending on him, he should show his sense of the favor of Providence by stepping out and leaving his chance to the younger men. Friend Lawrence did so—not to his own benefit ultimately, though that was no one's fault that ever I heard; and Martin Ludovic was his successor, and a great and honorable business was the outcome of his efforts. Now does thee happen to recall if Martin is a name in thy branch?"

"My grandfather was Martin Ludovic of the old New York house of Lawrence and Ludovic," said the cadet of that name; but as he gave these credentials a profound melancholy subdued his just and natural pride.

"Is it possible!" Friend Underhill exulted, more pleased than if he had recovered a lost bank-note for many hundreds. There are no people who hold by the ties of blood and family more strongly than the Friends; and Friend Underhill, on this long journey, had felt himself sadly insolvent in those sureties that cannot be packed in a trunk or invested in irrigable lands. It was as if on the wild, cold seas he had crossed the path of a bark from home. He yearned to have speech with this graciously favored young man, whose grandfather had been his Phebe's grandfather's partner and dearest friend. The memory of that connection had been cherished with ungrudging pride through the succeeding generations in which the Ludovics had gone up in the world and the Lawrences had come down. Friend Underhill did not recall—nor would he have thought it of the least importance—that a Lawrence had been the benefactor in the first place, and had set Martin Ludovic's feet upon the ladder of success. He took the young man's hand affectionately in his own, and studied the favor of his countenance.

"Thee has the family look," he said in a satisfied tone; "and they had no cause, as a rule, to be discontented with their looks."

Young Ludovic's eyes fell, and he blushed like a girl; the dark-red blood dyed his face with the color almost of shame. Phebe moved uneasily in her seat.

"Make room beside thee, Phebe," said her father; "or, no, friend Ludovic; sit thee here beside me. If the train should start, I could hear thee better. And thy name—let me see—thee must be a Charles Ludovic. In thy family there was always a Martin, and then an Aloys, and then a Charles; and it was said—though a foolish superstition, no doubt—that the king's name brought ill luck. The Ludovic whose turn it was to bear the name of the unhappy Stuart took with it the misfortunes of three generations."

"A very unjust superstition I should call it," pronounced Phebe.

"Surely, and a very idle one," her father acquiesced, smiling at her warmth. "I trust, friend Charles, it has been given thee happily to disprove it in thy own person."

"On the contrary," said Charles Ludovic, "if I am not the unluckiest of my name, I hope there may never be another."

He spoke with such conviction, such energy of sadness, only silence could follow the words. Then the old gentleman said, most gently and ruefully—

"If it be indeed as thee says, I trust it will not seem an intrusion, in one who knew thy family's great worth, to ask the nature of thy trouble—if by chance it might be my privilege to assist thee. I feel of rather less than my usual small importance—cast loose, as it were, between the old and the new; but if my small remedies should happen to suit with thy complaint, it would not matter that they were trifling—like Phebe's drops and pellets she puts such faith in," he added, with a glance at his daughter's downcast face.

"Dear sir, you *have* helped me, by the gift of the outstretched hand. Between strangers, as we are, that implies a faith as generous as it is rare."

"Nay, we are not strangers; no one of thy name shall call himself stranger to one of ours. Shall he, Phebe? Still, I would not importune thee—"

"I thank you far more than you can know; but we need not talk of my troubles. It was a graceless speech of mine to obtrude them."

"As thee will. But I deny the lack of grace. The gracelessness was mine to bring up a foolish saying, more honored in the forgetting."

Here Phebe interposed with a spoonful of the medicine her father had referred to so disparagingly. "I would not talk any more now, if I were thee, father. Thee sees how it makes thee cough."

At this, Ludovic rose to leave them; but Phebe detained him, shyly doing the honors of their quarters in the common caravan. He stayed, but a constrained silence had come upon him. The old gentleman closed his eyes, and sometimes smiled to himself as he sat so, beside the younger man, and Phebe had strange thoughts as she looked at them both. Her imagination was greatly stirred. She talked easily and with perfect unconsciousness to Ludovic, and told him little things she could remember having heard about the one generation of his family that had formerly been connected with her own. She knew more about it, it appeared, than he did. And more and more he seemed to lose himself in her eyes, rather than to be listening to her voice. He sat with his back to his companion across the aisle; at length the latter rose, and touched him on the shoulder. He turned instantly, and Phebe, looking up, caught the hard, roused expression that altered him into the likeness of another man.

"I am going outside." No more was said, but Ludovic rose, bowed to Phebe, and followed his curt fellow-passenger.

"What can be the connection between them?" thought the

girl. "They seem inseparable, yet not friends precisely. How could they be friends?" And in her prompt mental comparison the elder man inevitably suffered. She began to think of all the tragedies with which young lives are fatalistically bound up; but it was significant that none of her speculations included the possibility of anything in the nature of error in respect to this Charles Ludovic who called himself unhappy.

II

"Stop a moment. I want to speak to you," said Ludovic. The two men were passing through the gentlemen's toilet-room; Ludovic turned his back to the marble washstand, and waited, with his head up, and the tips of his long hands resting in his trousers' pockets. "I have a favor to ask of you, Mr. Burke."

"Well, sir, what's the size of it?"

"You must have heard some of our talk in there; you see how it is? They will never, of themselves, suspect the reason of your fondness for my company. Is it worth while, for the time we shall be together, to put them on to it? It's not very easy, you see; make it as easy as you can."

"Have I tried to make it hard, Mr. Ludovic?"

"Not at all. I don't mean that."

"Am I giving you away most of the time?"

"Of course not. You have been most awfully good. But you're—you're damnably in my way. I see you out of the corner of my eye always, when you aren't square in front of me. I can't make a move but you jump. Do you think I am such a fool as to make a break now? No, sir; I am going through with this; I'm in it most of the time. Now see here, I give you my word—and there are no liars of my name—that you will find me with you at Pocatello. Till then let me alone, will you? Keep your eyes off me. Keep out of range of my talk. I would like to say a word now and then without knowing there's a running comment in the mind of a man across the car, who thinks he knows me better than the people I am talking to—understand?"

"Maybe I do, maybe I don't," said Mr. Burke, deliberately. "I don't know as it's any of my business what you say to your friends, or what they think of you. All I'm responsible for is your person."

"Precisely. At Pocatello you will have my person."

"And have I got your word for the road between?"

"My word, and my thanks—if the thanks of a man in my situation are worth anything."

"I'm dum sorry for you, Mr. Ludovic, and I don't mind doing what little I can to make things easy"—Mr. Burke paused, seeing his companion smile. "Well, yes, I know it's hard—it's dooced almighty hard; and it looks like there was a big mistake somewheres, but it's no business of mine to say so. Have a cigar?"

Young Mr. Ludovic had accepted a number of Mr. Burke's palliative offers of cigars during their journey together; he accepted the courtesy, but he did not smoke the cigars. He usually gave them to the porter. He had an expensive taste in cigars, as in many other things. He paid for his high-priced preferences, or he went without. He was never willing to accept any substitute for the thing he really wanted; and it was very hard for him, when he had set his heart upon a thing, not to approach it in the attitude that an all-wise Providence had intended it for him.

About dusk the snow-plow engines from above came down for coal and water. They brought no positive word, only that the plows and shovelers were at work at both ends of the big cut, and they hoped the track would be free by daybreak. But the snow was still falling as night set in.

Ludovic and Phebe sat in the shadowed corner behind the curtains of No. 7. Phebe's father had gone to bed early; his cough was worse, and Phebe was treating him for that and for the fever which had developed as an attendant symptom. She was a devotee in her chosen school of medicine; she knew her remedies, within the limits of her household experience, and used them with the courage and constancy that are of no school, but which better the wisdom of them all.

Ludovic observed that she never lost count of the time through all her talk, which was growing more and more absorbing; he was jealous of the interruption when she said, "Excuse me," and looked at her watch, or rose and carried her tumblers of medicine alternately to the patient, and woke him gently; for it was now a case for strenuous treatment, and she purposed to watch out the night, and give the medicines regularly every hour.

Mr. Burke was as good as his word; he kept several seats distant from the young people. He had a private understanding, though, with the car officials: not that he put no faith in the word of a Ludovic, but business is business.

When he went to his berth about eleven o'clock he noticed that his prisoner was still keeping the little Quaker girl company, and neither of them seemed to be sleepy. The table where they had taken supper together was still between them, with Phebe's watch and the medicine tumblers upon it. The panel of looking-glass reflected the young man's profile, touched with gleams of lamplight, as he leaned forward with his arms upon the table.

Phebe sat far back in her corner, pale and grave; but when her eyes were lifted to his face they were as bright as winter stars.

It was Ludovic's intention, before he parted with Phebe, to tell her his story—his own story; the newspaper account of him she would read, with all the world, after she had reached Volney. Meantime he wished to lose himself in a dream of how it might have been could he have met this little Phebe, not on a side-track, his chance already spoiled, but on the main line, with a long ticket, and the road clear before them to the Golden Gate.

Under other circumstances she might not have had the same overmastering fascination for him; he did not argue that question with himself. He talked to her all night long as a man talks to the woman he has chosen and is free to win, with but a single day in which to win her; and underneath his impassioned tones, shading and deepening them with tragic meaning, was the truth he was withholding. There was no one to stand between Phebe and this peril, and how should she know whither they were drifting?

He told her stories of his life of danger and excitement and contrasts, East and West; he told her of his work, his ambitions, his disappointments; he carried her from city to city, from camp to camp. He spoke to sparkling eyes, to fresh, thrilling sympathies, to a warm heart, a large comprehension, and a narrow experience. Every word went home; for with this girl he was strangely sure of himself, as indeed he might have been.

And still the low music of his voice went on; for he did not lack that charm, among many others—a voice for sustained and moving speech. Perhaps he did not know his own power; at all events, he was unsparing of an influence the most deliberate and enthralling to which the girl had ever been subjected.

He was a Ludovic of that family her own had ever held in highest consideration. He was that Charles Ludovic who had called himself unhappiest of his name. Phebe never forgot this fact, and in his pauses, and often in his words, she felt the tug of that strong undertow of unspoken feeling pulling him back into depths where even in thought she could not follow him.

And so they sat face to face, with the watch between them

ticking away the fateful moments. For Ludovic, life ended at Pocatello, but not for Phebe.

What had he done with that faith they had given him—the gentle, generous pair! He had resisted, he thought that he was resisting, his mad attraction to this girl—of all girls the most impossible to him now, yet the one, his soul averred, most obviously designed for him. His wild, sick fancy had clung to her from the moment her face had startled him, as he took his last backward look upon the world he had forfeited.

His prayer was that he might win from Phebe, before he left her at Pocatello, some sure token of her remembrance that he might dwell upon and dream over in the years of his buried life.

It would not have been wonderful, as the hours of that strange night flew by, if Phebe had lost a moment, now and then, had sometimes wandered from the purpose of her vigil. Her thoughts strayed, but they came back duly, and she was constant to her charge. Through all that unwholesome enchantment her hold upon herself was firm, through her faithfulness to the simple duties in which she had been bred.

Meanwhile the train lay still in the darkness, and Ludovic thanked God, shamelessly, for the snow. How the dream outwore the night and strengthened as morning broke gray and cold, and quiet with the stillness of the desert, we need not follow. More and more it possessed him, and began to seem the only truth that mattered.

He took to himself all the privileges of her protector; the rights, indeed—as if he could have rights such as belong to other men, now, in regard to any woman.

If the powers that are named of good or evil, according to the will of the wisher, had conspired to help him on, the dream could not have drawn closer to the dearest facts of life; but no spells were needed beyond those which the reckless conjurer himself possessed—his youth, his implied misfortunes, his unlikeness to any person she had known, his passion, "meek, but wild," which he neither spoke nor attempted to conceal.

And Phebe sat like a charmed thing while he wove the dream about her. She could not think; she had nothing to do while her father slept; she had nowhere to go, away from this new friend of her father's choosing. She was exhausted with watching, and nervously unstrung. Her hands were ice; her color went and came; her heart was in a wild alarm. She blushed almost as she breathed, with his eyes always upon her; and blushing, could have wept, but for the pride that still was left her in this strange, unwholesome excitement.

It was an ordeal that should have had no witnesses but the angels; yet it was seen of the porter and the conductor and Mr. Burke. The last was not a person finely cognizant of situations like this one; but he felt it and resented it in every fibre of his honest manhood.

"What's Ludovic doing?" he asked himself in heated

soliloquy. "He's out of the running, and the old man's sick abed, and no better than an old woman when he's well. What's the fellow thinking of?"

Mr. Burke took occasion to ask him, when they were alone together—Ludovic putting the finishing touches to a shave; the time was not the happiest, but the words were honest and to the point.

"I didn't understand," said Mr. Burke, "that the little girl was in it. Now, do you call it quite on the square, Mr. Ludovic, between you and her? I don't like it, myself; I don't want to be a party to it. I've got girls of my own."

Ludovic held his chin up high; his hands shook as he worked at his collar-button.

"Have you got any boys?" he flung out in the tone of a retort.

"Yes; one about your age, I should guess."

"How would you like to see him in the fix I'm in?"

"I couldn't suppose it, Mr. Ludovic. My boy and you ain't one bit alike."

"Are your girls like her?"

"No, sir; they are not. I ain't worrying about them any, nor wouldn't if they was in her place. But there's points about this thing—"

"We'll leave the points. Suppose, I say, your boy was in my fix: would you grudge him any little kindness he might be able to cheat heaven, we'll say, out of between here and Pocatello?"

"Heaven can take care of itself; that little girl is not in heaven yet. And there's kindnesses and kindnesses, Mr. Ludovic. There are some that cost like the mischief. I expect you're willing to bid high on kindness from a nice girl, about now; but how about her? Has kindness gone up in her market? I guess not. That little creetur's goods can wait; she'd be on top in any market. I guess it ain't quite a square deal between her and you."

Ludovic sat down, and buried his hands in his pockets. His face was a dark red; his lips twitched.

"Are you going to stick to your bargain, or are you not?" he asked, fixing his eyes on a spot just above Mr. Burke's head.

"You've got the cheek to call it a bargain! But say it was a bargain. I didn't know, I say, that the little girl was in it. Your bank's broke, Mr. Ludovic. You ought to quit business. You've got no right to keep your doors open, taking in money like hers, clean gold fresh from the mint."

"O Lord!" murmured Ludovic; and he may have added a prayer for patience with this common man who was so pitilessly in the right. A week ago, and the right had been easy to him. But now he was off the track; every turn of the wheels tore something to pieces.

"There are just two subjects I cannot discuss with you," he said, sinking his voice. "One is that young lady. Her father knows my people. She shall know me before I leave her. They say we shall go through to-night. You must think I am the devil if you think that, without the right even to dispense with your company, I can have much to answer for between here and Pocatello."

"You are as selfish as the devil, that's what I think; and the worst of it is, you look as white as other folks."

"Then leave me alone, or else put the irons on me. Do one thing or the other. I won't be dogged and watched and hammered with your infernal jaw! You can put a ball through me, you can handcuff me before her face; but my eyes are my own, and my tongue is my own, and I will use them as I please."

Mr. Burke said no more. He had said a good deal; he had covered the ground, he thought. And possibly he had some sympathy, even when he thought of his girls, with the young fellow who had looked too late in the face of joy and gone clean wild over his mischance.

It was his opinion that Ludovic would "get" not less than twenty-five years. There were likely to be Populists on that jury; the prisoner's friends belonged to a clique of big monopolists; it would go harder with him than if he had been an honest miner, or a playful cow-boy on one of his monthly "tears."

When Ludovic returned to his section, Phebe had gone to sleep in the corner opposite, her muff tucked under one flushed cheek; the other cheek was pale. Shadows as delicate as the tinted reflections in the hollow of a snow-drift slept beneath her chin, and in the curves around her pathetic eyelids, and in the small incision that defined her pure red under lip. Again the angels, whom we used to believe in, were far from this their child.

Ludovic drew down all the blinds to keep out the glare, and sat in his own place, and watched her, and fed his aching dream.

He did not care what he did, nor who saw him, nor what anybody thought.

In the afternoon he took her out for a walk. The snow had stopped; her father was up and dressed, and very much better, and Phebe was radiant. Her sky was clearing all at once. She charged the porter to call her in "just twenty minutes," for then she must give the medicine again. On their way out of the car Ludovic slipped a dollar into the porter's hand. Somehow that clever but corrupted functionary let the time slip by, to Phebe's innocent amazement. Could he have gone to sleep? Surely it must be more than twenty minutes since they had left the car.

"He's probably given the dose himself," said Ludovic. "A good porter is always three parts nurse."

"But he doesn't know which medicine to give."

"Oh, let them be," he said impatiently. "He's talking to your father, and making him laugh. He'll brace him up better than any medicine. They will call you fast enough if you are needed."

They walked the platform up and down in front of the section-house. They were watched, but Ludovic did not care for that now.

"Will you take my arm?"

She hesitated, in amused consideration of her own inexperience.

"Why, I never *did* take any one's arm that I remember. I don't think I could keep step with thee."

The intimate pronoun slipped out unawares.

"I will keep step with *thee*."

"I don't know that I quite like to hear you use that word."

"But you used it, just now, to me."

"It was an accident, then."

"Your father says 'thee' to me."

"He is of an older generation; my mother wore the Friends' dress. But those customs had a religious meaning for them to which I cannot pretend. With me it is a sort of instinct; I can't explain it, nor yet quite ignore it."

"Have I offended that particular instinct of yours which attaches to the word 'thee'?"

He seemed deeply chagrined. He was one who did not like to make mistakes, and he had no time to waste in apologizing and recovering lost ground.

"People do say it to us sometimes in fun, not knowing what the word means to us," said Phebe.

In the fresh winter air she was regaining her tone—escaping from him, Ludovic felt, into her own sweet, calm self-possession.

"Then you distinctly refuse me whatever—the least—that word implies? I am one of those who 'rush in'?"

"Oh, no; but you are much too serious. It is partly a habit of speech; we cannot lose the habit of speaking to each other as strangers in three days."

"You were never a stranger to me. I knew you from the first moment I saw you; yet each moment since you have been a fresh surprise."

"I cannot keep up with you," she said, slipping her hand out of his arm. In the grasp of his passionate dream he was striding along regardless, not of her, but of her steps.

"Oh, little steps," he groaned within himself—"oh, little doubting steps, why did we not meet before?"

Oh, blessed hampering steps, how much safer would his have gone beside them!

"What a charming pair!" cried a lady passenger from the forward sleeper. She too was walking, with her husband, and her eye had been instantly taken by the gentle girl with the delicate wild-rose color, halting on the arm of a splendid youth with dare-devil eyes, who did not look as happy as he ought with that sweet creature on his arm.

"Isn't it good to know that the old stories are going on all the same?" said the sentimental traveler. "What do you say—will that story end in happiness?"

"I say that he isn't good enough for her," the husband replied.

"Then he'll be sure to win her," laughed the lady. "He has won her, I believe," she added more seriously, watching the pair where they stood together at the far end of the platform; "but something is wrong."

"Something usually is at that stage, if I remember. Come, let us get aboard."

The sun was setting clear in the pale saffron west. The train from the buried cut had been released, and now came sliding down the track, welcomed by boisterous salutations. Behind were the mighty snow-plow engines, backing down, enwreathed and garlanded with snow.

"A-a-all aboard!" the conductor drawled in a colloquial tone to the small waiting group upon the platform.

Slowly they crept back upon the main track, and heavily the motion increased, till the old chant of the rails began again, and they were thundering westward down the line.

III

Phebe was much occupied with her father, perhaps purposely so, until his bed-time. She made him her innocent refuge. Ludovic kept subtly away, lest the friendly old gentleman should be led into conversation, which might delay the hour of his retiring. He went cheerfully to rest about the time the lamps were lighted, and Phebe sought once more her corner in the empty section, shaded by her father's curtains.

Ludovic, dropping his voice below the roar of the train, asked if he might take the seat beside her.

He took it, and turned his back upon the car. He looked at his watch. He had just three hours before Pocatello. The train was making great speed; they would get in, the conductor said, by eleven o'clock. But he need not tell her yet. Half an hour passed, and his thoughts in the silence were no longer to be borne.

She was aware of his intense excitement, his restlessness, the nervous action of his hands. She shrank from the burning misery in his questioning eyes. Once she heard him whisper under his breath; but the words she heard were, "*My love! my love!*" and she thought she could not have heard aright. Her trouble increased with her sense of some involuntary strangeness in her companion, some recklessness impending which she might not know how to meet. She rose in her place, and said tremulously that she must go.

"Go!" He sprang up. "Go where, in Heaven's name? Stay," he implored, "and be kind to me! We get off at Pocatello."

"We?" she asked with her eyes in his.

"That man and I. I am his prisoner."

She sank down again, and stared at him mutely.

"He is the sheriff of Bingham County, and I am his prisoner," he repeated. "Do the words mean nothing to you?" He paused for some sign that she understood him. She dropped her eyes; her face had become as white as a snowdrop.

"He is taking me to Pocatello for the preliminary examination—oh, must I tell you this? If I thought you would never read it in the ghastly type—"

"Go on," she whispered.

"Examination," he choked, "for—for homicide. I don't know

what the judge will call it; but the other man is dead, and I am left to answer for the passion of a moment with my life. And you will not speak to me?"

But now she did speak. Leaning forward so that she could look him in the eyes, she said—

"I thought when I saw that man always with you, watching you, that he might be taking you, with your consent, to one of those places where they treat persons for—for unsoundness of the mind. I knew you had some trouble that was beyond help. I could think of nothing worse than that. It haunted me till we began to speak together; then I knew it could not be; now I wish it had been."

"I do not," said Ludovic. "I thank God I am not mad. There is passion in my blood, and folly, perhaps, but not insanity. No; I am responsible."

She remained silent, and he continued defensively—

"But I am not the only one responsible. Can you listen? Can you hear the particulars? One always feels that one's own case is peculiar; one is never the common sinner, you know.

"I have a friend at Pocatello; he is my partner in business. Two years ago he married a New York girl, and brought her out there to live. If you knew Pocatello, you would know what a privilege it was to have their house to go to. They made me free of it, as people do in the West. There is nothing they could not have asked of me in return for such hospitality; it was an obligation not less sacred on my part than that of family.

"When my friend went away on long journeys, on our common business, it was my place in his absence to care for all that was his. There are many little things a woman needs a man to do for her in a place like Pocatello; it was my pride and privilege to be at all times at the service of this lady. She was needlessly grateful, but she liked me besides: she was one who showed her likes and dislikes frankly. She had grown up in a small, exclusive set of persons who knew one another's grandfathers, and were accustomed to say what they pleased inside; what outsiders thought did not matter. She had not learned to be careful; she despised the need of it. She thought Pocatello and the people there were a joke. But there is a serious side even to Pocatello: you cannot joke with rattlesnakes and vitriol and slow mines. She made enemies by her gay little sallies, and she would never condescend to explain. When people said things that showed they had interpreted her words or actions in a stupid or a vulgar way, she gave the thing up. It was not her business to adapt herself to such people; it was theirs to understand her. If they could not, then it did not matter what they thought. That was her theory of life in Pocatello.

"One night I was in a place—not for my pleasure—a place where a lady's name is never spoken by a gentleman. I heard her name spoken by a fool; he coupled it with mine, and laughed. I walked out of the place, and forgot what I was there for till I found myself down the street with my heart jumping. That time I did right, you would say.

"But I met him again. It was at the depot at Pocatello. I was seeing a man off—a stranger in the place, but a friend of my friends; we had dined at their house together. This other—I think he had been drinking—I suppose he must have included me in his stupid spite against the lady. He made his fool speech again. The man who was with me heard him, and looked astounded. I stepped up to him. I said—I don't know what. I ordered him to leave that name alone. He repeated it, and I struck him. He pulled a pistol on me. I grabbed him, and twisted it out of his hand. How it happened I cannot tell, but there in the smoke he lay at my feet. The train was moving out. My friend pulled me aboard. The papers said I ran away. I did not. I waited at Omaha for Mr. Burke.

"And there I met you, three days ago; and all I care for now is just to know that you will not think of me always by that word."

"What word?"

"Never mind; spare me the word. Look at me! Do I seem to you at all the same man?"

Phebe slowly lifted her eyes.

"Is there nothing left of me? Answer me the truth. I have a right to be answered."

"You are the same; but all the rest of it is strange. I do not see how such a thing could be."

"Can you not conceive of one wild act in a man not inevitably always a sinner?"

"Oh, yes; but not that act. I cannot understand the impulse to take a life."

"I did not think of his miserable life; I only meant to stop his talking. He tried to take mine. I wish he had. But no, no; I should have missed this glimpse of you. Just when it is too late I learn what life is worth."

"Do men truly do those things for the sake of women? Were you thinking of your friend's wife when you struck him?"

"I was thinking of the man—what a foul-mouthed fool he was—not fit to"—He stopped, seeing the look on Phebe's face.

"Oh, I'm impossible, I know, to one like you! It's rather hard I should have to be compared, in your mind, to a race of men like your father. Have you never known any other men?"

"I have read of all the men other people read of. I have some imagination."

"I suppose you read your Bible."

"Yes: the men in the Bible were not all of the Spirit; but they worshiped the Spirit—they were humble when they did wrong."

"Did women ever love them?"

Phebe was silent.

"Do not talk to me of the Spirit," Ludovic pleaded. "I am a long way from that. At least I am not a hypocrite—not yet. Wait till I am a 'trusty,' scheming for a pardon. Can you not give me one word of simple human comfort? There are just forty minutes more."

"What can I say?"

"Tell me this—and oh, be careful! Could you, if it were permitted a criminal like me to expiate his sin in the world among living men, in human relations with them—could we ever meet? Could you say 'thee' to me, not as to an afflicted person or a child? Am I to be only a text, another instance—"

"Many would not blame you. Neither do I blame you, not knowing that life or those people," said Phebe. "But there was One who turned away from the evil-speakers, and wrote upon the sand."

"But those evil-speakers spoke the truth."

"Can a lie be stopped by a pistol-shot? But we need not argue."

"No; I see how it is. I shall be to you only another of the wretched sons of Cain."

"I am thy sister," she said, and gave him her hand.

He held it in his strong, cold, trembling clasp.

"Darling, do you know where I am going? I shall never see you, never again—unless you are like the sainted women of your faith who walked the prisons, and preached to them in bonds."

"Thy bonds are mine: but I am no preacher."

The drowsy lights swayed and twinkled, the wheels rang on the frozen rails as the wild, white wastes flew by.

"Father shall never know it," Phebe murmured. "He shall never know, if I can help it, why you called yourself unhappy."

"Is it such an unspeakable horror to you?" He winced.

"He has not many years to live; it would only be one

disappointment more." She was leaning back in her seat; her eyes were closed; she looked dead weary, but patient, as if this too were life, and not more than her share.

"Has your father any money, dear?"

She smiled: "Do we look like people with money?"

"If they would only let me have my hands!" he groaned. "To think of shutting up a great strong fellow like me—"

It was useless to go on. He sat, bitterly forecasting the fortunes of those two lambs who had strayed so far from the green pastures and still waters, when he heard Phebe say softly, as if to herself—

"We are almost there."

Mr. Burke began to fold his newspapers and get his bags in order. His hands rested upon the implements of his office—he carried them always in his pockets—while he stood balancing himself in the rocking car, and the porter dusted his hat and coat.

The train dashed past the first scattered lights of the town.

"Po-catello!" the brakeman roared in a voice of triumph, for they were "in" at last.

The porter came, and touched Ludovic on the shoulder.

"Gen'leman says he's ready, sir."

He rose and bent over Phebe. If she had been like any other girl he must have kissed her, but he dared not. He had prayed for a sign, and he had won it—that look of dumb and lasting anguish in her childlike eyes.

Yet, strange passion of the man's nature, he was not sorry for what he had done.

Mr. Burke took his arm in silence, and steered him out of the car; both doors were guarded, for he had feared there might be trouble. He was surprised at Ludovic's behavior.

"What's the matter with him?" the car-conductor asked, looking after the pair as they walked up the platform together. "Is he sick?"

"Mashed," said the porter, gloomily; for Ludovic had forgotten the parting fee. "Regular girl mash, the worst I ever saw."

"He's late about it, if he expects to have any fun," said the conductor; and he began to dance, with his hands in his great-coat pockets, for the night air was raw. He was at the end of his run, and was going home to his own girl, whom he had married the week before.

* * *

Friends and family influence mustered strong for Ludovic at the trial six weeks later. His lawyer's speech was the finest effort, it was said, ever listened to by an Idaho jury. The ladies went to hear it, and to look at the handsome prisoner, who seemed to grow visibly old as the days of the trial went by.

But those who are acquainted with the average Western jury need not be told that it was not influence that did it, nor the lawyer's eloquence, nor the court's fine-spun legal definitions, nor even the women's tears. They looked at the boy, and thought of their own boys, or they looked inside, and thought of themselves;

and they concluded that society might take its chances with that young man at large. They stayed out an hour, out of respect to their oath, and then brought in a verdict of "Not guilty;" and the audience had to be suppressed.

But after the jury's verdict there is society, and all the tongues that will talk, long after the tears are dry. And then comes God in the silence—and Phebe.

* * *

The men all say she is too good for him, whose name has been in everybody's mouth. They say it, even though they do not know the cruel way in which he won her love. But the women say that Phebe, though undeniably a saint (and "the sweetest thing that ever lived"), is yet a woman, incapable of inflicting judgment upon the man she loves.

The case is in her hands now. She may punish, she may avenge, if she will; for Ludovic is the slave of his own remorseless conquest. But Phebe has never discovered that she was wronged. There is something in faith, after all; and there is a good deal in blood, Friend Underhill thinks. "Doubtless the grandson of Martin Ludovic must have had great provocation."

A TOUCH OF SUN

I

The five-o'clock whistle droned through the heat. Its deep, consequential chest-note belonged by right to the oldest and best paying member of the Asgard group, a famous mining property of northern California.

The Asgard Company owned a square league of prehistoric titles on the western slope of the foot-hills—land enough for the preservation of a natural park within its own boundaries where fire-lines were cleared, forest-trees respected, and roads kept up. Wherever the company erected a board fence, gate, or building, the same was methodically painted a color known as "monopoly brown." The most conspicuous of these objects cropped out on the sunset dip of the property where the woods for twenty years had been cut, and the Sacramento valley surges up in heat and glare, with yearly visitations of malaria.

Higher than the buildings in brown, a gray-shingled bungalow ranged itself on the lap of its broad lawns against a slope of orchard tops climbing to the dark environment of the forest. Not the original forest: of that only three stark pines were left, which rose one hundred feet out of a gulch below the house and lent their ancient majesty to the modern uses of electric wires and telephone lines. Their dreaming tops were in the sky; their feet were in the sluicings of the stamp-mill that reared its long brown back in a semi-recumbent posture, resting one elbow on the hill; and beneath the valley smouldered, a pale mirage by day, by night a vision of color transcendent and rich as the gates of the Eternal City.

At half past five the night watchman, on his way from town, stopped at the superintendent's gate, ran up the blazing path, and thrust a newspaper between the dark blue canvas curtains that shaded the entrance of the porch. For hours the house had slept behind its heat defenses, every shutter closed, yards of piazza blind and canvas awning fastened down. The sun, a ball of fire, went slowly down the west. Rose-vines drooped against the hanging lattices, printing their watery lines of split bamboo with a shadow-pattern of leaf and flower. The whole house-front was decked with dead roses, or roses blasted in full bloom, as if to celebrate with appropriate insignia the passing of the hottest day of the year.

Half-way down the steps the watchman stopped, surprised by a voice from behind the curtains. He came back in answer to his name.

A thin white hand parted the curtain an inch or two. There was the flicker of a fan held against the light.

"Oh, Hughson, will you tell Mr. Thorne that I am here? He doesn't know I have come."

"Tell him that Mrs. Thorne is home?" the man translated slowly.

"Yes. He does not expect me. You will tell him at once, please?"

"Yes, ma'am."

The curtain was fastened again from inside. A woman's step went restlessly up and down, up and down the long piazza floors, now muffled on a rug, now light on a matting, or distinct on the bare boards.

Later a soft Oriental voice inquired, "Wha' time Missa Tho'ne wanta dinna?"

"The usual time, Ito," came the answer; "make no difference for me."

"Lika tea—coffee—after dinna?"

"Tea—iced. Have you some now? Oh, bring it, please!"

After an interval: "Has Mr. Thorne been pretty well?"

"I think."

"It is very hot. How is your kitchen—any better than it was?"

"Missa Tho'ne fixa more screen; all open now, thank you."

"Take these things into my dressing-room. No; there will be no trunk. I shall go back in a few days."

The gate clashed to. A stout man in a blaze of white duck came up the path, lifting his cork helmet slightly to air the top of his head. As he approached it could be seen that his duck was of a modified whiteness, and that his beard, even in that forcing weather, could not be less than a two days' growth. He threw his entire weight on the steps one by one, as he mounted them slowly. The curtains were parted for him from within.

"Well, Margaret?"

"Well, dear old man! How hot you look! *Why* do you not carry an umbrella?"

"Because I haven't got you here to make me. What brought you back in such weather? Where is your telegram?"

"I did not telegraph. There was no need. I simply had to speak to you at once—about something that could not be written."

"Well, it's good to have a look at you again. But you are going straight back, you know. Can't take any chances on such weather as this."

Mr. Thorne sank copiously into a piazza chair, and pulled forward another for his wife.

She sat on the edge of it, smiling at him with wistful satisfaction. Her profile had a delicate, bird-like slant. Pale, crisped auburn hair powdered with gray, hair that looked like burnt-out ashes, she wore swept back from a small, tense face, full of fine lines and fleeting expressions. She had taken off her high, close neckwear, and the wanness of her throat showed above a collarless shirt-waist.

"Don't look at me; I am a wreck!" she implored, with a little exhausted laugh. "I wonder where my keys are? I must get on something cool before dinner."

"Ito has all the keys somewhere. Ito's a gentleman. He takes beautiful care of me, only he won't let me drink as much *shasta* as I want. What is that? Iced tea? Bad, bad before dinner! I'm going to watch *you* now. You are not looking a bit well. Is there any of that decoction left? Well, it is bad; gets on the nerves, too much of it. The problem of existence here is, What shall we drink, and how much of it *can* we drink?"

Mrs. Thorne laughed out a little sigh. "I have brought you a problem. But we will talk when it is cooler. Don't you—don't you shave but twice a week when I am away, Henry?"

"I shave every day, when I think of it. I never go anywhere, and I don't have anybody here if I can possibly avoid it. It is all a man can do to live and be up to his work."

"I know; it's frightful to work in such weather. How the mill roars! It starts the blood to hear it. Last spring it sounded like a cataract; now it roars like heat behind furnace doors. Which is your room now?"

"O Lord! I sleep anywhere; begin in my bed generally and end of the piazza floor. It will be the grass if this keeps on."

"Mrs. Thorne continued to laugh spasmodically at her husband's careless speeches, not at what he said so much as through content in his familiar way of saying things. Under their light household talk, graver, questioning looks were exchanged, the unappeased glances of friends long separated, who realize on meeting again that letters have told them nothing.

"Why didn't you write me about this terrible heat?"

"Why didn't you write *me* that you were not well?"

"I am well."

"You don't look it—anything but."

"I am always ghastly after a journey. It isn't a question of health that brought me. But—never mind. Ring for Ito, will you? I want my keys."

At dinner she looked ten years younger, sitting opposite him in her summery lawns and laces. She tasted the cold wine soup, but ate nothing, watching her husband's appetite with the mixed wonder and concern that thirty years' knowledge of its capacities had not diminished. He studied her face meanwhile; he was accustomed to reading faces, and hers he knew by line and precept. He listened to her choked little laughs and hurried speeches. All her talk was mere postponement; she was fighting for time. Hence he argued that the trouble which had sent her flying home to him from the mountains was not fancy-bred. Of her imaginary troubles she was ready enough to speak.

The moon had risen, a red, dry-weather moon, when they walked out into the garden and climbed the slope under low orchard boughs. The trees were young, too quickly grown; like child mothers, they had lost their natural symmetry, overburdened with hasty fruition. Each slender parent trunk was the centre of a host of artificial props, which saved the sinking boughs from breaking. Under one of these low green tents they stopped and handled the great fruit that fell at a touch.

"How everything rushes to maturity here! The roses blossom and wither the same hour. The peaches burst before they ripen. Don't you think it oppresses one, all this waste fertility, such an excess of life and good living, one season crowding upon another? How shall we get rid of all these kindly fruits of the earth?"

She did not wait for an answer to her morbid questions. They moved on up a path between hedges of sweet peas going to seed, and blackberry-vines covered with knots of fruit dried in their own juices. A wall of gigantic Southern cane hid the boundary fence, and above it the night-black pines of the forest towered, their breezy monotone answering the roar of the hundred stamps below the hill.

A few young pines stood apart on a knoll, a later extension of the garden, ungraded and covered with pine-needles. In the hollow places native shrubs, surprised by irrigation, had made an unwonted summer's growth.

Here, in the blanching moon, stood a tent with both flaps thrown back. A wind of coolness drew across the hill; it lifted one of the tent-curtains mysteriously; its touch was sad and searching.

Mrs. Thorne put back the canvas and stepped inside. She

saw a folding camp-cot stripped of bedding, a dresser with half-open drawers that disclosed emptiness, a dusty book-rack standing on the floor. The little mirror on the tent-pole, hung too high for her own reflection, held a darkling picture of a pine-bough against a patch of stars. She sat on the edge of the cot and picked up a discarded necktie, sawing it across her knee mechanically to free it from the dust. Her husband placed himself beside her. His weight brought down the mattress and rocked her against his shoulder; he put his arm around her, and she gave way to a little sob.

"When has he written to you?" she asked. "Since he went down?"

"I think so. Let me see! When did you hear last?"

"I have brought his last letter with me. I wondered if he had told you."

"I have heard nothing—nothing in particular. What is it?"

"The inevitable woman."

"She has come at last, has she? Come to stay?"

"He is engaged to her."

Mr. Thorne breathed his astonishment in a low whistle. "You don't like it?" he surmised at once.

"Like it! If it were merely a question of liking! She is impossible. She knows it, her people know it, and they have not told him. It remains—"

"What is the girl's name?"

"Henry, she is not a girl! That is, she is a girl forced into premature womanhood, like all the fruits of this hotbed climate. She is that Miss Benedet whom you helped, whom you saved—how many years ago? When Willy was a schoolboy."

"Well, she *was* saved, presumably."

"Saved from what, and by a total stranger!"

"She made no mistake in selecting the stranger. I can testify to that; and she was as young as he, my dear."

"A girl is never as young as a boy of the same age. She is a woman now, and she has taken his all—everything a man can give to his first—and told him nothing!"

"Are you sure it's the same girl? There are other Benedets."

"She is the one. His letter fixes it beyond a question—so innocently he fastens her past upon her! And he says, 'She is "a woman like a dewdrop."' I wonder if he knows what he is quoting, and what had happened to *that* woman!"

"Dewdrops don't linger long in the sun of California. But she was undeniably the most beautiful creature this or any other sun ever shone on."

"And he is the sweetest, sanest, cleanest-hearted boy, and the most innocent of what a woman may go through and still be fair outside!"

"Why, that is why she likes him. It speaks well for her, I think, that she hankers after that kind of a boy."

"It speaks volumes for what she lacks herself! Don't misunderstand me. I hope I am not without charity for what is done and never can be undone—though charity is hardly the virtue one would hope to need in welcoming a son's wife. It is her ghastly silence now that condemns her."

Mr. Thorne heaved a sigh, and changed his feet on the gritty tent floor. He stooped and picked up some small object on which he had stepped, a collar-stud trodden flat. He rolled it in his fingers musingly.

"She may be getting up her courage to tell him in her own time and way."

"The time has gone by when she could have told him honorably. She should have stopped the very first word on his lips."

"She couldn't do that, you know, and be human. She couldn't be expected to spare him at such a cost as that. Mighty few men would be worth it."

"If he wasn't worth it she could have let him go. And the family! Think of their accepting his proposal in silence. Why, can they even be married, Henry, without some process of law?"

"Heaven knows! I don't know how far the other thing had gone—far enough to make questions awkward."

Husband and wife remained seated side by side on the son's deserted bed. The shape of each was disconsolately outlined to the other against the tent's illumined walls. Now a wind-swayed branch of manzanita rasped the canvas, and cast upon it shadows of its moving leaves.

"It's pretty rough on quiet old folks like us, with no money to get us into trouble," said Mr. Thorne. "The boy is not a beauty, he's not a swell. He is just a plain, honest boy with a good working education. If you judge a woman, as some say you can, by her choice of men, she shouldn't be very far out of the way."

"It is very certain you cannot judge a man by his choice of women."

"You cannot judge a boy by the women that get hold of him. But Willy is not such a babe as you think. He's a deuced quiet sort, but he's not been knocking around by himself these ten years, at school and college and vacations, without picking up an idea or two—possibly about women. Experience, I grant, he probably lacks; but he has the true-bred instinct. We always have trusted him so far; I'm willing to trust him now. If there are things he ought to know about this woman, leave him to find them out for himself."

"After he has married her! And you don't even know whether a marriage is possible without some sort of shuffling or concealment; do you?"

"I don't, but they probably do. Her family aren't going to get themselves into that kind of a scrape."

"I have no opinion whatever of the family. I think they would accept any kind of a compromise that money can buy."

"Very likely, and so would we if we had a daughter—"

"Why, we *have* a daughter! It is our daughter, all the daughter we shall ever call ours, that you are talking about. And to think of the girls and girls he might have had! Lovely girls, without a flaw—a flaw! She will fall to pieces in his hand. She is like a broken vase put together and set on the shelf to look at."

"Now we are losing our sense of proportion. We must sleep on this, or it will blot out the whole universe for us."

"It has already for me. I haven't a shadow of faith in anything left."

"And I haven't read the paper. Suppose the boy were in Cuba now!"

"I wish he were! It is a judgment on me for wanting to save him up, for insisting that the call was not for him."

"That's just it, you see. You have to trust a man to know his own call. Whether it's love or war, he is the one who has got to answer."

"But you will write to him to-morrow, Henry? He must be saved, if the truth can save him. Think of the awakening!"

"My dear, if he loves her there will be no awakening. If there is, he will have to take his dose like other men. There is nothing in the truth that can save him, though I agree with you that he ought to know it—from her."

"If you had only told her your name, Henry! Then she would have had a fingerpost to warn her off our ground. To think what you did for her, and how you are repaid!"

"It was a very foolish thing I did for her; I wasn't proud of it. That was one reason why I did not tell her my name."

Mr. Thorne removed his weight from the cot. The warped wires twanged back into place.

"Come, Maggie, we are too old not to trust in the Lord—or something. Anyhow, it's cooler. I believe we shall sleep to-night."

"And haven't I murdered sleep for you, you poor old man? What a thing it is to have nerve and no nerves! I know you feel just as wrecked as I do. I wish you would say so. I want it said to the uttermost. If I could but—our only boy—our boy of 'highest hopes'! You remember the dear old Latin words in his first 'testimonials'?"

"They must have been badly disappointed in their girl, and I suppose they had their 'hopes,' too."

"They should not drag another into the pit, one too innocent to have imagined such treachery."

"I wouldn't make too much of his innocence. He is all right so far as we know; he's got precious little excuse for not being: but there is no such gulf between any two young humans; there can't be, especially when one is a man. Take my hand. There's a step there."

Two shapes in white, with shadows preposterously lengthening, went down the hill. The long, dark house was open now to the night.

* * *

There is no night in the "stilly" sense at a mine.

The mill glared through all its windows from the gulch. Sentinel lights kept watch on top. The hundred stamps pounded on. If they ceased a moment, there followed the sob of the pump, or the clang of a truck-load of drills dumped on the floor of the hoisting-works, or the thunder of rock in the iron-bound ore-bins. All was silence on the hill; but a wakeful figure wrapped in white went up and down the empty porches, light as a dead leaf on the wind. It was the mother, wasting her night in grievous thinking, sighing with weariness, pining for sleep, dreading the day. How should they presume to tell that woman's story, knowing her only through one morbid chapter of her earliest youth, which they had stumbled upon without the key to it, or any knowledge of its sequel? She longed to feel that they might be merciful and not tell it. She coveted happiness for her son, and in her heart was prepared for almost any surrender that would purchase it for him. If the lure were not so great! If the woman were not so blinding fair, why, then one might find a virtue in excusing her, in condoning her silence, even. But, clothed in that power, to have pretended innocence as well!

The roar of the stamp-heads deadened her hearing of the night's subtler noises. Her thoughts went grinding on, crushing the hard rock of circumstance, but incapable of picking out the grains of gold therein. Later siftings might discover them, but she was reasoning now under too great human pressure for delicate analysis.

She saw the planets set and the night-mist cloak the valley. By four o'clock daybreak had put out the stars. She went to her room then and fell asleep, awakening after the heat had begun, when the house was again darkened for the day's siege.

She was still postponing, wandering through the darkened rooms, peering into closets and bureau drawers to see, from force of habit, how Ito discharged his trust.

At luncheon she asked her husband if he had written. He made a gesture expressing his sense of the hopelessness of the situation in general.

"You know how I came by my knowledge, and how little it amounts to as a question of facts."

"Henry, how can you trifle so! You believe, just as I do, that such facts would wreck any marriage. And you are not the only one who knows them. I think your knowledge was providentially given you for the saving of your son."

"My son is a man. *I* can't save him. And take my word for it, he will go all lengths now before he will be saved."

"Let him go, then, with his eyes open, not blindfold, in jeopardy of other men's tongues."

Mr. Thorne rose uneasily.

"Do as you think you must; but it rather seems to me that I am bound to respect that woman's secret."

"You wish that you had not told me."

"Well, I have, and I suppose that was part of the providence. It is in your hands now; be as easy on her as you can."

With a view to being "easy," Mrs. Thorne resolved not to expatiate, but to give the story on plain lines. The result was hardly as merciful as might have been expected.

* * *

"DEAR WILLY," she wrote: "Prepare yourself for a most unhappy letter [what woman can forego her preface?]—unhappy mother that I am, to have such a message laid upon me.

But you will understand when you have read why the cup may not pass from us. If ever again a father or a mother can help you, my son, you have us always here, poor in comfort though we are. It seems that the comforters of our childhood have little power over those hurts that come with strength of years.

"Seven years ago this summer your father went to the city on one of his usual trips. Everything was usual, except that at Colfax he noticed a pair of beautiful thoroughbred horses being worked over by the stablemen, and a young fellow standing by giving directions. The horses had been overridden in the heat. It was such weather as we are having now. The young man, who appeared to have everything to say about them, was of the country sporting type, distinctly not the gentleman. In a cattle country he would have been a cowboy simply. Your father thought he might have been employed on some of the horse-breeding ranches below Auburn as a trainer of young stock. He even wondered if he could have stolen the animals.

"But as the train moved out it appeared he had appropriated something of greater value—a young girl, also a thoroughbred.

"It did not need the gossip of the train-hands to suggest that this was an elopement of a highly sensational kind. Father was indignant at the jokes. You know it is a saying with the common sort of people that in California elopements become epidemic at certain seasons of the year—like earthquake shocks or malaria. The man was handsome in a primitive way—worlds beneath the girl, who was simply and tragically a lady. Father sat in the same car with them, opposite their section. It grew upon him by degrees that she was slowly awakening, as one who has been drugged, to a stupefied consciousness of her situation. He thought there might still be room for help at the crisis of her return to reason (I mean all this in a spiritual sense), and so he kept near them. They talked but little together. The girl seemed stunned, as I say, by physical exhaustion or that dawning comprehension in which your father fancied he recognized the tragic element of the situation.

"The young man was outwardly self-possessed, as horsemen are, but he seemed constrained with the girl. They had no conversation, no topics in common. He kept his place beside her, often watching her in silence, but he did not obtrude himself. She appeared to have a certain power over him, even in her helplessness, but it was slipping from her. In her eyes, as they rested upon him in the hot daylight, your father believed that he saw a wild and gathering repulsion. So he kept near them.

"The train was late, having waited at Colfax two hours for the Eastern Overland, else they would have been left, those two, and your father—but such is fate!

"It was ten o'clock when they reached Oakland. He lost the pair for a moment in the crowd going aboard the boat, but saw the girl again far forward, standing alone by the rail. He strolled across the deck, not appearing to have seen her. She moved a trifle nearer; with her eyes on the water, speaking low as if to herself, she said—

"'I am in great danger. Will you help me? If you will, listen, but do not speak or come any nearer. Be first, if you can, to go ashore; have a carriage ready, and wait until you see me. There will be a moment, perhaps—only a moment. Do not lose it. You understand? *He,* too, will have to get a carriage. When he comes for me I shall be gone. Tell the driver to take me to—' she gave the number of a well-known residence on Van Ness Avenue.

"He looked at her then, and said quietly, 'The Benedet house is closed for the summer.'

"She hung her head at the name. 'Promise me your silence!' she implored in the same low, careful voice.

"'I will protect you in every way consistent with common sense,' your father answered, 'but I make no promises.'

"'I am at your mercy,' she said, and added, 'but not more than at his.'

"'Is this a case of conspiracy or violence?' your father asked.

"She shook her head. 'I cannot accuse him. I came of my own free will. That is why I am helpless now.'

"'I do not see how I can help you,' said father.

"'You can help me to gain time. One hour is all I ask. Will you or not?' she said. 'Be quick! He is coming.'

"'I must go with you, then,' your father answered, 'I will take you to this address, but I need not tell you the house is empty.'

"'There are people in the coachman's lodge,' she answered. Then her companion approached, and no more was said.

"But the counter-elopement was accomplished as only your

father could manage such a matter on the spur of the moment—consequences accepted with his usual philosophy and bonhomie. If he could have foreseen *all* the consequences, he would not, I think, have refused to give her his name.

"He left her at the side entrance, where she rang and was admitted by an oldish, respectable looking man, who recognized her evidently with the greatest surprise. Then your father carried out her final order to wire Norwood Benedet, Jr., at Burlingame, to come home that night to the house address and save—she did not say whom or what; there she broke off, demanding that your father compose a message that should bring him as sure as life and death, but tell no tales. I do not know how she may have put it—these are my own words.

"There was a paragraph in one newspaper, next morning, which gave the girl's full name, and a fancy sketch of her elopement with the famous range-rider Dick Malaby. This was just after the close of the cattlemen's war in Wyoming. Malaby had fought for one of the ruined English companies. (The big owners lost everything, as you know. The country was up in arms against them; they could not protect their own men.) Malaby's employers were friends of the Benedets, and had asked a place with them for their liegeman. He was a desperado with a dozen lives upon his head, but men like Norwood Benedet and his set would have been sure to make a pet of him. One could see how it all had come about, and what a terrible publicity such a name associated with hers would give a girl for the rest of her life.

"But money can do a great deal. Society was out of town; the newspapers that society reads were silent.

"It was announced a few days later that Mrs. Benedet and her daughter Helen had gone East on their way to Europe. As Mr. Benedet's health was very bad—this was only six months before he died—society wondered; but it has been accustomed to wondering about the Benedets.

"Mrs. Benedet came home at the time of her husband's death and remained for a few months, but Helen was kept away. You know they have continually been abroad for the last seven years, and Helen has never been seen in society here. When you spoke of 'Miss Benedet' I no more thought of her than if she had not been living. Aunt Frances met them last winter at Cannes, and Mrs. Benedet said positively that they had no intention of coming back to California ever to live. Aunt Frances wondered why, with their beautiful homes empty and going to destruction. I have told you the probable reason. Whether it still exists, God knows—or what they have done with that man and his dreadful knowledge.

"Helen Benedet may have changed her spiritual identity since she made that fatal journey, but she can hardly have forgotten what she did. She must know there is a man who, if he lives, holds her reputation at the mercy of his silence. Money can do a great deal, but it cannot do everything.

"I am tempted to wish that we—your father and I—could share your ignorance, could trust as you do. Better a common awakening for us all, than that I should be the one necessity has chosen to apply the torture to my son.

"The misery of this will make you hate my handwriting forever. But why do I babble? You do not hear me. God help you, my dear!"

* * *

These words, descriptive of her own emotions, Mrs. Thorne on re-reading scored out, and copied the last page.

She did not weep. She ached from the impossibility of weeping. She stumbled away from her desk, tripping in her long robes, and stretched herself out at full length on the floor, like a girl in the first embrace of sorrow. But hearing Ito's footsteps, she rose ashamed, and took an attitude befitting her years.

The letter was absently sealed and addressed; there was no reason why the shaft should not go home. Yet she hesitated. It were better that she should read it to her husband first.

The sun dropped below the piazza roof and pierced the bamboo lattices with lines and slits of fervid light.

"From heat to heat the day declined."

The gardener came with wet sacking and swathed the black-glazed jardinières, in which the earth was steaming. The mine whistle blared, and a rattle of miners' carts followed, as the day-shift dispersed to town. The mine did not board its proletariate. At his usual hour the watchman braved the blinding path, and left the evening paper on the piazza floor. There it lay unopened. Mrs. Thorne fanned herself and looked at it. There must be fighting in Cuba; she did not move to see. Other mothers' sons were dying; what was death to such squalor as hers? Sorrow is a queen, as the poet says, and sits enthroned; but Trouble is a slave. Mothers with griefs like hers must suffer in the fetters of silence.

When dinner was over, Ito made his nightly pilgrimage through the house, opening bedroom shutters, fastening curtains back. He drew up the piazza-blinds, and like a stage-scene, framed in post and balustrade, and bordered with a tracery of rose-vines, the valley burst upon the view. Its cool twilight colors, its river-bed of mist, added to the depth of distance. Against it the white roses looked whiter, and the pink ones caught fire from the intense, great afterglow.

The silent couple, drinking their coffee outside, drew a long mutual sigh.

"Every day," said Mrs. Thorne, "we wonder why we stay in such a place, and every evening we are cajoled into thinking there never can be such another day. And the beauty is just as fresh every night as the heat is preposterous by day."

"It's a great strain on the men," said Mr. Thorne. "We lost two of our best hands this week—threw down their tools and quit, for some tomfoolery they wouldn't have noticed a month ago. The bosses irritate the men, and the men get fighting mad in a minute. Not one of them will bear the weight of a word, and I don't blame them. The work is hard enough in decent weather; they are dropping off sick every day. The night-shift boys can't sleep in their hot little houses—they look as if they'd all been on a two weeks' tear. The next improvement we make I shall build a rest-house where the night-shift can turn in and sleep inside of stone walls, without crying babies and scolding wives clattering around. This heat every summer costs us thousands of dollars in delays, from wear and tear and extra strain—tempers and nerves giving out, men getting frantic and jerking things. I believe it breeds a form of acute mania when it keeps on like this."

"Yes, the point of view changes the instant the sun goes down," said Mrs. Thorne. "I am glad I did not send my letter. Will you let me read it to you, Henry?"

"Not now; let us enjoy the peace of God while it lasts." He stretched himself on his back on the rattan lounge, and folded his hands on that part of his person which illustrated, geographically speaking, the great Continental Divide. The locked hands rose softly up and down. His wife fanned him in silence.

He turned his head and looked at her; her tired eyes, the dragged lines about her mouth, disturbed his sense of rest. He took the fan from her and returned her attention vigorously. "Please don't!" she said with a little teased laugh. She rearranged the lock he had blown across her forehead. His larger help she needed, but he had seldom known how to pet her in little ways.

"I think you ought to let me read it to you," she said. "There is nothing so difficult as telling the truth, even about one's self, and when it's another person—"

"That's what I claim; she is the only one who can tell it."

"This is a case of first aid to the injured," she sighed. "I may not be a surgeon, but I must do what I can for my son."

Then there was silence; the valley grew dimmer, the sky nearer and more intense.

"Yes, the night forgives the day," after a while she said; "it even forgets. And we forget what we were, and what we did, when we were young. What is the use of growing old if we can't learn to forgive?" she vaguely pleaded; and suddenly she began to weep.

The rattle of a miner's cart broke in upon them; it stopped at the gate. Mr. Thorne half rose and looked out; a man was hurrying up the walk. He waved with his cane for him to stop where he was. Messengers at this hour were usually bearers of bad news, and he did not choose that his wife should know all the troubles of the mines.

The two men conversed together at the gate; then Mr. Thorne returned to explain.

"I must go over to the office a moment, and I may have to go to the power-house."

"Is anybody hurt?"

"Only a pump. Don't think of things, dear. Just keep cool while you can."

"For pity's sake, there is a carriage!" Mrs. Thorne exclaimed. "We are going to have a visitor. Fancy making calls after such a day as this!"

Mr. Thorne hurried away with manlike promptitude in the face of a social obligation. The mistress stepped inside and gave an order to Ito.

As she returned, a lady was coming up the walk. She was young and tall, and had a distant effect of great elegance. She held herself very erect, and moved with the rapid, swimming step peculiar to women who are accustomed to the eyes of critical assemblages. Her thin black dress was too elaborate for a country drive; it was a concession to the heat which yet permitted the wearing of a hat, a filmy creation supporting a pair of wings that started up from her beautiful head like white flames. But Mrs. Thorne chiefly observed the look of tense preparation in the face that met hers. She retreated a little from what she felt to be a crisis of some sort, and her heart beat hard with acute agitation.

"Mrs. Thorne?" said the visitor. "Do I need to tell you who I am? Has any one forewarned you of such a person as Helen Benedet?"

The two women clasped hands hurriedly. The worn eyes of the elder, strained by night-watchings, drooped under the young, dark ones, reinforced by their splendor of brows and lashes.

"It was very sweet of you to come," she said in a lifeless voice.

"Without an invitation! You did not expect me to be quite so sweet as that?"

Mrs. Thorne did not reply to this challenge. "You are not alone?" she asked gently.

"I am alone, dear Mrs. Thorne. I am everything I ought not to be. But you will not mind for an hour or two? It's a great deal to ask of you, this hot night, I know."

"You must not think of going back to-night." Mrs. Thorne glanced at the hired carriage from town. "Did you come on purpose, this dreadful weather, my dear? I am very stupid, but I've only just come myself."

"Oh, you are angelic! I heard at Colfax, as we were coming up, that you were at the mine. I came—by main strength. But I should have come somehow. Have you people staying with you? You look so very gay with your lights—you look like a whole community."

"We have no lights here, you see; we are anything but gay. We were talking of you only just now," Mrs. Thorne added infelicitously.

The other did not seem to hear her. She let her eyes rove down the lengths of empty piazza. The close-reefed awnings revealed the stars above the trees, dark and breezeless on the lawn. The matted rose-vines clung to the pillars motionless.

"What a strange, dear place!" she murmured. "And there is no one here?"

"No one at all. We are quite alone. We really must have you."

"I will stay, then. It's perfectly fearful, all I have to say to you. I shall tire you to death."

Ito, appearing, was ordered to send away the lady's carriage.

"May he bring me a glass of water? Just water, please." The tall girl, in her long black dress, moved to and fro, making a pretense of the view to escape observation.

"What is that sloping house that roars so? It sounds like a house of beasts. Oh, the stamps, of course! There goes one on the bare metal. Did anything break then?"

"Oh, no," said Mrs. Thorne; "things do not break so easily as that in a stamp-mill. Only the rock gets broken."

Ito returned with a tray of iced soda, and was spoken to aside by his mistress.

"It's quite a farce," she said, "preparing beds for our friends in this weather. No one sleeps until after two, and then it is morning; and though we shut out the heat, it beats on the walls and burns up the air inside, and we wake more tired than ever."

"Let us not think of sleep! I need all the night to talk in. I have to tell you impossible things."

"Is Willy's father to be included in this talk?" Mrs. Thorne inquired; "because he is coming—he is there, at the gate."

She rose uneasily. Her visitor rose, too, and together they watched the man's unconscious figure approaching. An electric lamp above the gate threw long shadows, like spokes of a wheel, across the grass. Mr. Thorne's face was invisible till he had reached the steps.

"Henry," said his wife, "you do not see we have a visitor."

He took off his hat, and perceiving a young lady, waved her a gallant and playful greeting, assuming her to be a neighbor. Miss Benedet stepped back without speaking.

"God bless me!" said Thorne simply, when his wife had named their guest, and so left the matter, for Miss Benedet to acknowledge or deny their earlier meeting.

Mrs. Thorne gave her little coughing laugh.

"Well, you two!" she said with ghastly gayety. "Must I repeat, Henry, that this is—"

"He is trying to think where he has seen me before," said Helen Benedet. There was a ring in her voice like that of the stamp-heads on the bare steel.

"I am wondering if you remember where you saw me before," Thorne retorted. He did not like the young lady's presence there. He thought it extraordinary and rather brazen. And he liked still less to be drawn into a woman's parlance.

Mrs. Thorne sat still, trembling. "Henry, tell her! Speak to her!"

Miss Benedet turned from husband to wife. Her face was very pale. "Ah," she said, "you knew about me all the time! He has told you everything—and you called me 'my dear'! Is it easy for you to say such things?"

"Never mind, never mind! What did you wish to say to me? What was it?"

"Give me a moment, please! This alters everything. I must get accustomed to this before we go any further."

She reached out her white arm with the thin sleeve wrinkled over it, and helped herself again to water. In every gesture there was the poise and distinction of perfect self-command, a highly wrought self-consciousness, as far removed from pose as from Nature's simplicity. Natural she could never be again. No woman is natural who has a secret experience to guard, whether of grief or shame, her own or of any belonging to her.

"You are the very man," she said, "the one who would not promise. And you kept your word and told your wife. And how long have you known of—of this engagement?"

Mr. Thorne looked at his wife.

"Only a few days," she said.

"Still, there has been time," the girl reflected. She let her voice fall from its high society pitch. "I did not dream there was so much mercy in the world—among parents! You both knew, and you have not told him. You deserve to have Willy for your son!"

Mrs. Thorne leaned forward to speak. Her husband, guessing what trouble her conscience would be making her, forestalled the effort with a warning look. "There was no mercy in the case," he bluntly said; "we do not know your story."

Miss Benedet continued, as if thinking aloud: "Yet you gave me that supreme trust, that I would tell him myself! I have not, and now it is too late. Now I can never know how he would have taken it had he known in time. I do not want his forgiveness, you may be sure, or his toleration. I must be what I was to him or nothing. You will tell him, and then he will understand the letter I wrote him last night, breaking the engagement. We may be honest with each other now; there is no peace of the family to provide for. This night's talk, and I leave myself, my whole self, with you, to do with as you think best for him. If you think better to have it over at one blow, tell him the worst. The facts are enough if you leave out the excuses. But if you want to soften it for the sake of his faith in general—isn't there some such idea, that men lose their faith in all women through the fault of one?—why, soften it all you like. Make me the victim of circumstances. I can show you how. I had forgiven myself, you know. I thought I was as good as new. I had forgotten I had a flaw. And I was so tired of being on the defensive. Now at last, I said, I shall have a friend! You know—*do* you know what a restful, impersonal manner your son has? What quiet eyes! We rode and talked together like two young men. It seems a pleasure common enough with some girls, but I never had it; lads of my own age were debarred when I was a girl. I had neither girls nor boys to play with. Girl friends were dealt out to me to fit my supposed needs, but taken that way as medicine I didn't find them very interesting. If I clung to one more than another, that one was not asked soon again for fear of inordinate affections and unbalanced enthusiasms. I was to be an all-around young woman; so they built a wall all around me. It fitted tight at last, and then I broke through one night and emptied my heart on the ground. My plea, you see, is always ready. Could I have lived and kept on scorning myself as I did that night? Do you remember?" She bent her imperative, clears gaze upon Thorne. "I told you the truth when you gave me a chance to lie. Heaven knows what it cost to say, 'I came with him of my own free will!'"

Mrs. Thorne put her hand in her husband's. He pressed it absently, with his eyes on the ground.

"It is such a mercy that I need not begin at the beginning. You know the worst already, and your divine hesitation before judgment almost demands that I should try to justify it. I *may* excuse myself to you. I will not be too proud to meet you half-way; but remember, when you tell the story to him, everything is to be sacrificed to his cure."

"When we really love them," Mrs. Thorne unexpectedly argued, "do we want them to be cured?"

The defendant looked at her in astonishment, "Do I understand you?" she asked. "You must be careful. I have not told you my story. Of course I want to influence you, but nothing can alter the facts."

There was no reply, and she took up her theme again with visible and painful effort. A sickening familiarity, a weariness of it all before she had begun, showed in her voice and in her pale, reluctant smile.

"Seven years is a long time," she said, looking at Thorne. "Are you sure you have forgotten nothing? You saw what the man was?" she demanded. "He was precisely what he looked to be—one of the men about the stables. I was not supposed to know one from another.

"It is a mistake to talk of a girl having fallen. She has crawled down in her thoughts, a step at a time—unless she fell in the dark; and I declare that before this happened it was almost dark with me!

"My mother is a very clever woman; she has had the means to carry out her theories, and I am her only child (Norwood Benedet is my half-brother). I was not allowed to play with ordinary children; they might have spoiled my accent or told me stories that would have made me afraid of the dark; and while the perfect child was waited for, I had only my nurses. I was not allowed to go to school, of course. Schools are for ordinary children. When I was past the governess age I had tutors, exceptional beings, imported like my frocks. They were too clever for the work of teaching one ignorant, spoiled child. They wore me out with their dissertations, their excess of personality, their overflow of acquirements, all bearing upon poor, stupid me, who could absorb so little. And mama would not allow me to be pushed, so I never actually worked or played. These persons were in the house, holidays and all, and there was a perpetual little dribble of instruction going on. Oh, how I wearied of the deadly deliberation of it all!

"As a family we have always been in a way notorious; I am aware of that: but my mother's ideals are far different from those that held in father's young days, when he made his money and a highly ineligible circle of acquaintances. Nordy inherited all the fun and the friends, and he spent the money like a prince. Once or twice a year he would come down to the ranch, and the place would be filled with his company, and their horses and jockeys and servants. Then mama would fly with me till the reign of sport was over. It was a terrible grief to have to go at the only time when the ranch was not a prison. I grew up nursing a crop of smothered rebellions and longings which I was ashamed to confess. At sixteen mama was to take me abroad for two years; I was to be presented and brought home in triumph, unless Europe refused to part with a pearl of such price. All pearls have their price. I was not left in absolute ignorance of my own. Of all who suffered through that night's madness of mine, poor mama is most to be pitied. There was no limit to her pride in me, and she has never made the least pretense that religion or philosophy could comfort her.

"Now, before I really begin, shall we not speak of something else for a while? I do not want to be quite without mercy."

"I think you had better go on," said Mrs. Thorne gently; "but take off your bonnet, my dear."

"Still 'my dear'?" sighed the girl. "Is so much kindness quite consistent with your duty? Will you leave *all* the plain speaking to me?"

"Forgive me," said the mother humbly; "but I cannot call you 'Miss Benedet.' We seem to have got beyond that."

"Oh, we have got beyond everything! There is no precedent for us in the past"—she felt for her hat pins—"and no hope in the future." She put off the winged circlet that crowned her hair, and Mrs. Thorne took it from her. Almost shyly the middle-aged woman, who had never herself been even pretty, looked at the sad young beauty, sitting uncovered in the moonlight.

"You should never wear anything on your head. It is desecration."

"Is it? I always conform, you know. I wear anything, do anything, that is demanded."

"Ah, but the head—such hair! I wonder that I do not hate you when I think of my poor Willy."

"You will hate me when I am gone," said the beautiful one wearily; "you may count on the same revulsion in him. I know it. I have been through it. There is nothing so loathsome in the bitter end as mere good looks."

"Ah, but why"—the mother checked herself. Was she groveling already for Willy's sake? She had stifled the truth, and accepted thanks not her due, and listened to praise of her own magnanimity. Where were the night's surprises to leave her?

II

Mr. Thorne had changed his seat, and the sound of a fresh chair creaking under his comfortable weight was a touch of commonplace welcomed by his wife with her usual laugh, half amused and half apologetic.

"Why do you go off there, Henry? Do you expect us to follow you?"

"There's a breeze around the corner of the house!" he ejaculated fervently.

"Go and find it, then; we do not need you. Do we?"

"*I* need him," said the girl in her sweetest tones. "He helped me once, without a word. It helps me now to have him sitting there—"

"Without a word!" Mrs. Thorne irrepressibly supplied.

"Why can't we let her finish?" Thorne demanded, hitching his chair into an attitude of attention.

It was impossible for Miss Benedet to take up her story in the key in which she had left off. She began again rather flatly, allowing for the chill of interruptions—

"To go back to that summer; I was in my sixteenth year, and the policy of expansion was to have begun. But father's health broke, and mama was traveling with him and a cortège of nurses, trying one change after another. It was duller than ever at the ranch. We sat down three at table in a dining-room forty feet long, Aunt Isabel Dwight, Fräulein Henschel, and myself. Fräulein was the resident governess. She was a great, soft-hearted, injudicious creature, a mass of German interjections, but she had the grand style on the piano. There had been weeks of such weather as we are having now. Exercise was impossible till after sundown. I had dreamed of a breath of freedom, but instead of the open door I was in straiter bonds than ever.

"I revolted first against keeping hours. I would not get up to breakfast, I refused to study, it was too hot to practice. I took my own head about books, and had my first great orgy of the Russians. I used to lie beside a chink of light in the darkened library and read while Fräulein in the music-room held orgies of her own. She had just missed being a great singer; but she was a master of her instrument, and her accompaniments were divine. What voice she had was managed with feeling and a pure method, and where voice failed her the piano thrilled and sobbed, and broke in chords like the sea.

"I can give you no idea of the effect that Tolstoi, combined with Fräulein's music, had upon me. My heart hung upon the pauses in her song; it beat, as I read, as if I had been running. I would forget to breathe between the pages. One day Fräulein came in and found me in the back chapters of 'Anna Karénina.' She had been playing one of Lizst's rhapsodies—the twelfth. Waves of storm and passion had been thundering through the house, with keen little rifts of melody between, too sweet almost to be endured. She was very negligée, as the weather obliged us to be. Her great white arms were bare above the elbow, and as wet as if she had been over the wash-tub.

"'That is not a book for a *jeune fille*,' she said.

"I was in a rapture of excitement; the interruption made me wild. 'All the books are for me,' I told her. 'I will read what I please.'

"'You will go mad!'

"I went on reading.

"'You have no way to work it off. You will not study, you cannot sing, you write no letters, the mother does not believe—'

"'Do go away!' I cried.

"'—in the duty to the neighbor. Ach! what will you do with the whole of Tolstoi and Turgenieff shut up within you?'

"'I can ride,' I said. 'If you don't want me to go mad, leave me in the evenings to myself. Take my place in the carriage with

Aunt Isabel, and let me ride alone.'

"Fräulein had lived in bonds herself, and she had the soul of an artist. She knew what it is, for days together, to have barely an hour to one's own thoughts; never to step out alone of a summer night, after a long, hot, feverish day. She let me go with old Manuel, the head groom, as my escort. He was no more hindrance to solitude than a pine-tree or a post.

"The reading and the music and the heat went on. I was in a fever of emotion such as I had never known. Fräulein perceived it. She recommended 'My Religion' as an antidote to the romances. I did not want his religion. I wanted his men and women, his reading of the human soul, the largeness of incident, the sense of time and space, the intricacy of family life, the problems of race, the march of nations across the great world-canvas.

"I rode—not alone, but with the high-strung beings that lived between the pages of my books: men and women who knew no curb, who stopped at nothing, and who paid the price of their passionate mistakes. Old Manuel, standing by the horses, looked strange to me. I spoke to him dramatically, as the women I read of would have spoken. Nothing could have added to or detracted from his own manner. He was of the old Spanish stock, but for the first time I saw his picturesqueness. I liked him to call me 'the Niña,' and address me in the third person with his eyes upon the ground.

"All this was preparatory. It is part of my defense; but do not forget the heat, the imprisonment, the sense of relief when the sun went down, the wild, bounding rapture of those night rides.

"One evening it was not Manuel who stood by the horses in the white track between the laurels. It was a figure as statuesque as his, but younger, and the pose was not that of a servant. It was the stand-at-ease of a soldier, or of an Indian wrapped in his blanket in the city square. This man was conscious of being looked at, but his training, of whatever sort, would not permit him to show it. Plainly the training had not been that of a groom. I was obliged to send him to the stables for his coat, and remind him that his place was behind. He took the hint good-humoredly, with the nonchalance of a big boy condescending to be taught the rules of some childish game. As we were riding through the woods later, I caught the scent of tobacco. It was my groom smoking. I told him he could not smoke and ride with me. He threw away his cigarette and straightened himself in the saddle with such a smile as he might have bestowed on the whims of a child. He obeyed me exactly in everything, with an exaggerated ironical precision, and seemed to find amusement in it. I questioned him about Manuel. He had gone to one of the lower ranches, would not be back for weeks. By whose orders was he attending me? By Manuel's, he said. He must then have had qualifications.

"'What is one to call you?' I asked him.

"He hesitated an instant. 'Jim is what I answer to around here,' said he.

"'What is your *name?*' I repeated.

"'The lady can call me anything she likes,'—he spoke in a low, lazy voice,—'but Dick Malaby is my name.'

"We have better heroes now than the Cheyenne cowboys, but I felt as a girl to-day would feel if she discovered she had been telling one of the men of the Merrimac to ride behind!"

"They would not need to be told," Mrs. Thorne interjected.

"No, that is the difference; but discipline did not appeal to me then; recklessness did. Every man on the place had taken sides on the Wyoming question; feeling ran high. Some of them had friends and relatives among the victims. Yet this man in hiding had tossed me his name to play with, not even asking for my silence, though it was the price of his life, and all in a light-hearted contempt for the curious ways of the 'tony set,' as he would have called us.

"I signed to him one evening to ride up. 'I want you to talk to me,' I said. 'Tell me about the cattle war.'

"'Miss Benedet forgets—my place is behind.' He touched his hat and fell back again. Lesson for lesson—we were quits. I made no further attempt to corrupt my own pupil.

"We rode in silence after that, but I was never without the sense of his ironical presence. I was conscious of showing off before him. I wished him to see that I could ride. Fences and ditches, rough or smooth, he never interfered with my wildest pace. I could not extract from him a look of surprise, far less the admiration that I wanted. What was a girl's riding to him? He knew a pace—all the paces—that I could never follow. I felt the absurdity of our mutual position, its utter artificiality, and how it must strike him.

"In the absence of words between us, externals spoke with greater force. He had the Greek line of head and throat, and he sat his horse with a dare-devil repose. The eloquence of his mute attitudes, his physical mastery of the conditions, his strength repressed, tied to my silly freaks and subject to my commands, while his thoughts roamed free! That was the beginning. It lasted through a week of starlight and a week of moonlight—lyric nights with the hot, close days between; and each night an increasing interest attached to the moment when he was to put me on my horse. I make no apology for myself after that.

"One evening we approached a gate at the farther end of our longest course, and the gate stood open. He rode on to close it. I stopped him. 'I am going out,' I said. It was a resolution taken that moment. He held up his watch to the light, which made me angry.

"'Go back to the stables,' I said, 'if you are due there. *I* don't want to know the time.'

"He brought his horse alongside. 'Where is Miss Benedet going, please?'

"'Anywhere,' I said, 'where it will be cool in the morning.'

"'Miss Benedet will have a long ride. Does she wish for company?'

"I did not answer. Something drove me forward, though I was afraid.

"'Outside that gate,' he went on quietly, '*I* shall set the pace, and I do not ride behind.' Still I did not answer. 'Is that the understanding?'

"'Ride where you please,' I said.

"After that he took command, not roughly or familiarly, but he no longer used the third person, as I had instructed him, in speaking to me. The first time he said 'you' it sent the blood to my face. We were far up the mountain then, and morning was upon us.

"I wish to be definite here. From the moment I saw him plainly face to face the illusion was gone. Before, I had seen him by every light but daylight, and generally in profile. The profile is not the man. It is the plan in outline, but the eyes, the mouth, tell what he has made of himself. So attitude is not speech. As a shape in the moonlight he had been eloquent, but once at my side, talking with me naturally—I need not go on! From that moment our journey was to me a dream of horror, a series of frantic plans for escape.

"All fugitives on the coast must put to sea. The Oakland ferry would have answered my purpose. I would never have been seen with him in the city—alive.

"But at Colfax we met your husband. He knows—you know—the rest."

* * *

In thinking of the one who had first pitied her, pity for herself overcame her, and the proud penitent broke down.

Mr. and Mrs. Thorne sat in the shy silence of older persons who are past the age of demonstrative sympathy. The girl rose, and as she passed her hostess she put out her hand. Mrs. Thorne took it quickly and followed her. They found a seat by themselves in a dark corner of the porch.

"Your poor, good husband—how tired he is! How patiently you have listened, and what does it all come to?"

"Think of yourself, not of us," said Mrs. Thorne.

"Oh, it's all over for me. I have had my fight. But you have *him* to grieve for."

"Shall you not grieve for him yourself a little?"

The girl sat up quickly.

"If you mean do I give him up without a struggle—I do not. But you need not say that to him. I told him that it was all a mistake; I did not—do not love him."

"How could you say that—"

"It was necessary. Without that I should have been leaving it to his generosity. Now it remains only to show him how little he has lost."

"But could you not have done that without belying yourself? You do—surely you still care for him a little?"

"Insatiate mother! Is there any other proof I can give?"

"Your hand is icy cold."

"And my face is burning hot. Good-night. May I say, 'Now let thy servant depart in peace'?"

"I shall not know how to let you go to-morrow, and I do not see, myself, why you should go."

"You will—after I am gone."

"My dear, are you crying? I cannot see you. How cruel we have been, to sit and let you turn your life out for our inspection!"

"It was a free exhibition! No one asked me, and I did not even come prepared, more than seven years' study of my own case has prepared me.

"I was a child; but the fault was mine. I should have been allowed to suffer for it in the natural way. No good ever comes of skulking. But they hurried me off to Europe, and began a cowardly system of concealment. They made me almost forget my own misconduct in shame for the things they did by way of covering it up. My mother never took me in her arms and cried over my disgrace. She would not speak of it, or allow me to speak. Not a word nor an admission; the thing must be as though it had never been!

"They ruined Dick Malaby with their hush-money. They might better have shot him, but that would have made talk. My father died with only servants around him. Mama could not go to him. She was too busy covering my retreat. Oh, she kept a gallant front! I admired her, I pitied her, but I loathed her policy. Does not every girl know when she has been dedicated to the great god Success, and what the end of success must be?

"I told mama at last that if she would bring men to propose to me I should tell them the truth. Does Lord So-and-so wish to marry a girl who ran away with her father's groom? That was the breach between us. She has thrown herself into it. She is going to marry a title herself, not to let it go out of the family. Have you not heard of the engagement? She is to be a countess, and the property is controlled by her, so now I have an excuse for doing something."

"My dear!" Mrs. Thorne took the girl's cold hands in hers. "Do you mean that you are not your father's heiress?"

"Only by mama's last will and testament. We know what that would be if she made it now!"

"It was *then* you came home?"

"It was then, when I learned that one of my rejected suitors was to become my father. He might be my grandfather. But let us not be vulgar!"

"Aren't you girls going to bed to-night?" Mr. Thorne inquired, with his usual leaning toward peace and quietness. "You can't settle everything at one sitting."

"Everything is settled, Mr. Thorne, and I am going to bed," said Miss Benedet.

Mrs. Thorne did not release her hands. "I want to ask you one more question."

"I know exactly what it is, and I will tell you to-morrow."

"Tell me now; it is perfectly useless going to your room; the temperature over your bed is ninety-nine."

"The question, then! Why did I allow your son to commit himself in ignorance?"

"No, no!" Mrs. Thorne protested.

"Yes, yes! You have asked that question, you must have. You are an angel, but you are a mother, too."

"I have asked no questions since you began to tell your story; but I have wondered how Willy could have found courage, in one week, to offer himself to such gifts and possessions as yours."

"A mother, and a worldly mother!" Miss Benedet apostrophized. "I did not look for such considerations from you. And you are troubled for the modesty of your son?"

"My dear, he has nothing, and he is—of course we think him everything he should be—but he is not a handsome boy."

"Thank Heaven he is not."

"And he does not talk—"

"About himself. No."

"Ah, you do care for him! You understand him. You would—"

Miss Benedet rose to her feet with decision.

"You have not answered my question," the unconscionable mother pursued. "Does he know—is it known that you are not the great heiress your name would imply?"

"Everything is known," said the girl. "You do not read your society column, I see. Six weeks ago you might have learned the fate of my father's millions."

She stood by the balustrade and leaned out under the stars, taking a deep breath of the night's growing coolness. A rose-spray touched her face. She put it back, and a shower of dry, scented petals fell upon her breast and sleeve.

"There is always one point in every true story," she said in a tired voice, "where explanations cease to explain. The mysteries claim their share in us, deny them as we will. I don't know why it was, but from the time I threw off all that bondage to society and struck out for myself, I felt made over. Life began again with life's realities. I came home to earn my bread, and on that footing I felt sane and clean and honest. The question became not what I am or was, but what could I do? I discussed the question with your son."

"You discussed!"

"We did, indeed. We went over the whole field. East and west we tested my accomplishments by the standards of those who want teachers for their children. I have gone rather further in music than anything else. Even Fräulein would hardly say now I lacked an outlet. I was working things off one evening on the piano—many things beyond the power of speech—the help of prayer, I might say. There were whispers about me already in the house."

"What *do* you mean?"

"People talking—my mother's old friends. It was rather serious, as I had been thinking of their daughters for pupils. I thought I was alone, but your son—the 'boy' as you call him—was listening. He came and stood beside me. For a person who does not talk, he can make himself quite well understood. I tried to go on playing. My blinded eyes, the wrong notes, told him all. I lay and thought all night, and asked myself, why might I not be happy and give happiness, like other women of my age. I denied to my conscience that I was bound to tell him, since I was not, never had been, what that story in words would report me. Why should I affect a lie in order literally, vainly to be honest? So a day passed, and another sleepless night. And now I had his image of me to battle with. Then it became impossible, and yet more necessary, and each day's silence buried me deeper beyond the hope of speech. So I gave it up. Why should he have in his wife less than I would ask for in my husband? I want none of your experienced men. Such a record as his, such a look in the eyes, the expression unawares of a life of sustained effort—always in one direction—"

A white arm in a black sleeve pointed upward in silence.

"And you would rob him of his reward?" said the mother, in a choked voice.

"Mrs. Thorne! Do you not understand me? I am not talking for effect. But this is what happens if one begins to explain. I did not come here to talk to you for the rest of my life! It was your sweetness that undid me. I will never again say what I think of parents in general."

* * *

"Maggie, do you know what time it is?" a suppressed voice issued an hour later from that part of the house supposed to be dedicated to sleep. "Are you going to sit up till morning?"

"I am looking for my letter," came the answer, in a tragic whisper.

"What letter?"

"My letter to Willy, that you wouldn't let me read to you last night."

"You don't want to read it to me now, do you?"

There was no reply. A careful step kept moving about the inner rooms, newspapers rustled, and small objects were lifted and set down.

"Maggie, do come to bed! You can't mail your letter to-night."

"I don't want to mail it. I want to burn it. I will not have it on my conscience a moment longer—"

"I wish you'd have me on your conscience! It's after one o'clock." The voices were close together now, only an open door between the speakers.

"Won't you put something on and come out here, Henry? There is a light in Ito's house. I suppose you wouldn't let me go out and ask him?"

"I suppose not!"

"Then won't you go and ask if he saw a letter on my desk, sealed and addressed?"

Mr. Thorne sat up in bed disgustedly. "What is Ito doing with a light this time of night?"

"Hush, dear; don't speak so loud. He's studying. He's preparing himself to go into the Japanese navy."

"He is, is he! And that's why he can't get us our breakfast before half-past eight. I'll see about that light!"

"The letter, the letter!" Mrs. Thorne prompted in a ghostly—whisper. "Ask him if he saw it on my desk—a square blue envelope, thin paper."

The studious little cook was seated by a hot kerosene-lamp, at a table covered with picture-papers, soft Japanese books, and writing-materials. He was in his stocking-feet and shirt-sleeves, and his mental efforts appeared to have had a confusing effect on his usually sleek black hair, which stood all ways distractedly, while his sleepy eyes blinked under Mr. Thorne's brusque examination.

"I care fo' everything," he repeated, eliminating the consonants as he slid along. "Missa Tho'ne letta—all a-ready fo' mail—I putta pos'age-stamp, gifa to shif'-boss. I think Sa' F'a'cisco in a mo'ning. I care fo' everything!"

"Ito cares for everything," Mr. Thorne quoted, in answer to his wife's haggard inquiries. "He stamped your letter and sent it to town yesterday by one of the day-shift men."

"Now what shall be done!" Mrs. Thorne exclaimed tragically.

"I know what *I* shall do!" Mr. Thorne wrapped his toga around him with an air of duty done. But a husband cannot escape so easily as that. His ministering angel sat beside his bed for half an hour longer, brooding aloud over the day's disaster, with a rigid eye upon the question of personal accountability.

"If you had not stopped me, Henry, when I tried to confess about my letter! There's no time for the truth like the present."

"My dear, when a person is telling a story you don't want to interrupt with quibbles of conscience; if it made it any easier for her to think us a little better than we are, why rob her of the delusion?"

"I shall have to rob her of it to-morrow. To think of my sitting there, a whited sepulchre, and being called generous and forbearing and merciful, with that letter lying on my desk all the time!"

"It would be lying there still except for an accident. She will see how you feel about it. Give her something to forgive in you. Depend upon it, she'll rise to the occasion."

* * *

As the mother passed her guest's room next morning she paused and looked remorsefully at the closed door.

"I ought to have told her that we never shut our doors. She must be smothered. I wonder if she can be asleep."

Mr. Thorne went on into the dining-room. Mrs. Thorne knocked, in a whisper as it were. There was no answer. She softly unlatched the door, and a draft of air crept through, widening it with a prolonged and wistful creak. The sleeper did not stir. She had changed her pillows to the foot of the bed, and was lying in the full light, with her window-curtains drawn. In all the room there was an air of abandonment, an exhausted memory of the night's despairing heat. Mrs. Thorne stepped across the matting, and noiselessly bowed the shutters. A dash of spray from the lawn-sprinkler was spattering the sill, threatening to dampen a pile of dainty clothing laid upon a chair. She moved the chair, looked once more at the lovely dark-lashed sleeper, and left her again in peace.

Beside her plate at the breakfast-table there was a great heap of roses, gathered that morning, her husband's usual greeting. She praised them as she always did, and then began to finger them over, choosing the finest to save for her guest. Rare as they were in kind, and opened that morning, there was not a perfect rose among them. Each one showed the touch of blight in bloom. Every petal, just unclosed and dewy at the core, was curled along the edges, scorched in the bud. It was not mildew or canker or disease, only "a touch of sun."

"I won't give them to her," said the mother; "they are too like herself."

She saw her husband go forth into the heat again, and blamed herself, according to her wont of a morning after the night's mistakes, for robbing him of his rest and heaping her self-imposed burdens upon him. He laughed at the remorse tenderly, and brushed away the burdens, and faced the day's actualities with the not too fine remark, "I must go and see what's loose outside."

Everything was "loose" apparently. Something about a "hoist" had broken in the night, and the men were still at work without breakfast, an eighteen-hour shift. The order came for Ito to send out coffee and bread and fruit to the famished gang. Ito was in the lowest of spirits; had just given his mistress warning that he could not stay. The affair of the letter had wounded his susceptibilities; he must go where he would be better understood. All this in a soft, respectful undertone, his mistress trying to comfort him, and incidentally hasten his response to the requisition from outside. At eleven o'clock Mr. Thorne sent in a pencil message on a card: "I shall not be home to lunch. Does she want to get the 12:30 train?" Mrs. Thorne replied in the same manner, by bearer: "She did, but she is asleep. I don't like to wake her."

The darkened house preserved its silence, a restless endurance of the growing heat. Mrs. Thorne, in the thinnest of morning gowns, her damp hair brushed back from her powdered temples, sat alone at luncheon. Ito had put a melancholy perfection into his last salad. It was his valedictory.

She was about to rise when Miss Benedet came silently into the room with her long, even step. Her dark eyes were full of sleep. Mrs. Thorne rang, and began to fuss a little over her guest to cover the shyness each felt at the beginning of a new day. They had parted at too high a pitch of expression to meet again in the same emotional key.

Miss Benedet looked at the clock, lifting her eyebrows wearily. "I have lost my train," she remarked, but added no reproaches. "Is there an evening train to the city?"

"Not from here," Mrs. Thorne replied; "but we could send you over to Colfax to catch the night train from there. I hoped we could have you another day."

"That would be impossible," said Miss Benedet; "but I shall be giving you a great deal of trouble."

"Oh, no; it is only ten miles. Mr. Thorne will take you; we will both take you. It is a beautiful drive by moonlight through the woods. Was I wrong not to call you?"

"If you were, you will be punished by having me on your hands this long, hot afternoon. I ought to have gone last night. When one has parted with the very last bit of one's self, one should make haste to remove the shell."

"Then you would have left me with something remaining on my mind, something I must get rid of at once. Come, let us go where we cannot see each other's faces. I am deeply in the wrong concerning you."

Mrs. Thorne went on incriminating herself so darkly in her preface that when she came to the actual offense her confessor smiled. "I am so relieved!" she exclaimed. "This is much more like real life. I felt you must be keeping something back, or, if not, I could never live up to such a pitch of generosity. I am glad you did not reach it all at once."

"But what becomes of the truth—the story as it should have been told to Willy? Oh, I have sinned, for want of patience, of faith—not against you, dear, but my son!"

After a silence Miss Benedet said, "Now for the heart of my own weakness. Suppose that I did have a hope. Suppose that I had laid the responsibility upon you, the parents, hoping that you would decide for happiness, mere happiness, without question of desert or blame. And suppose you had defended me to him. Would that have been best? Where then would be his cure?

Now let us put away all cowardice, for him as well as for ourselves. Happiness for him could have but one foundation. You have told him the facts; if he cannot bear them as all the world knows them, that is his cure. I thank you. You knew where to put the knife."

"Oh, but this is cruel!" said the mother. "I don't want to be your judge. You have had your punishment, and you took it like a queen. Now let us think of Willy!"

"Please!" said the girl. "I cannot talk of this any more. We must stop sometime."

The time of twilight came; the gasping house flung open doors and windows to the night. Mr. Thorne pursued his evening walk alone among the fruits and vegetables, counting his egg-plants, and marking the track of gophers in his rows of artichokes. The women were strolling toward the hill. Miss Benedet had put on a cloth skirt and stiff shirt-waist for her journey, and suffered from the change, but did not show it. Her beauty was not of the florid or melting order. Mrs. Thorne regarded her inconsolably, noting with distinct and separate pangs each item of her loveliness, as she moved serene and pale against the dark, resonant green of the pines. They followed a foot-path back among the trees to a small gate or door in the high boundary fence. Mrs. Thorne tried it to see if it were locked.

"Willy used to live, almost, on this hill when he came out for his vacations." She spoke dreamily, as if thinking aloud. "He slept in that tent. It looks like a little ghost to me these nights in the moonlight, the curtains flap in such a lonely way. That gate was his back door through the woods to town. His wheel used to lean against this tree. I miss his fair head in the sun, and his white trousers springing up the hill. But one cannot keep one's boy forever. You have made him a man, my dear."

The mother put out her hand timidly. She had ventured on forbidden ground once more. But she was not rebuffed. The girl's hand clasped hers and drew it around a slender waist, and they walked like two school friends together.

"I cannot support the idea that you will never come again," mourned the elder. "It is years since I have known a girl like you—a girl who can say things. I can make no headway with girls in general. They are so big and silent and athletic. They wear pins and badges, and belong to more *things* than I have ever heard of!"

Miss Benedet laughed. "I am silent, too, sometimes," she said.

"But you are not dense!"

"I'm afraid you go very much to extremes in your likes and dislikes, dear lady, and you are much younger than I, you know."

"I am quite aware of that," said Mrs. Thorne. "You have had seven years of Europe to my twenty of Cathay."

"Dear Cathay!" the girl murmured, with moist eyes; "I could live in this place forever."

"Where have you lived? Tell me in how many cities of the world."

"Oh, we never lived. We stayed in places for one reason or another. We were two years in Vienna. I worked there. I was a pupil of Leschetizky."

"What!"

"Did I not tell you? I can play a little."

"A little! What does that exactly mean?"

"It means too much for drawing-room music, and not enough for the stage."

"You are not thinking of that, are you?"

"Why that voice of scorn? Have I hit upon one of your prejudices?"

"I am dreadfully old-fashioned about some things—publicity, for instance."

"It depends upon the kind, doesn't it? But you will never hear of me on the concert stage. Leschetizky says I have not the poise I might have had. He is very clever. There was a shock, he says, to the nerve centres. They will never again be quite under control. It is true. At this moment I am shivering within me because I must say good-by to one I might have had all my life for a friend. Is it so?"

"My dear, if you mean me, I love you!"

"Call me Helen, then. You said 'my dear' before you knew me."

"Before I meant it."

* * *

"I wonder who can be arriving. That is the carriage I came out in last night."

A light surrey with two seats passed below the hill, and was visible an instant against a belt of sky.

"It is going to stop," said Mrs. Thorne. "Suppose we step back a little. I shall not see visitors to-night. Very likely it is only some one for Mr. Thorne."

A tall young man in traveling clothes stepped out upon the horse-block, left his luggage there, and made ten strides up the walk. They heard his step exploring the empty piazzas.

"It is Willy!" said Mrs. Thorne in a staccato whisper.

"Then good-by!" said Miss Benedet. "I will find Mr. Thorne in the garden. Dearest Mrs. Thorne, you must let me go!"

"You will not see him? Not see Willy!"

"Not for worlds. He must not know that I am here. I trust you." She tore herself away.

Mrs. Thorne stood paralyzed between the two—her advancing son, and her fleeing guest.

"Willy!" she cried.

Her tall boy was bending over her—once more the high, fair head, the smooth arch of the neck, which she could barely reach to put her arms about it.

"Mother!" The word in his grave man's voice thrilled her as once had the touch of his baby hands.

"I am afraid to look at you, my son. How is it with you?"

"I am all right, mother. How are things here?"

"Oh, don't speak of us! Did you get my letter?"

"This morning."

"And you read it, Willy?"

"Of course."

There was a silence. Mrs. Thorne clasped her son's arm and leaned her head against it.

"I am sorry you worried so, mother."

"What does it matter about me?"

"I am sorry you took it so hard—because—I knew it all the time."

"You knew it! What do you mean?"

"A nice old lady told me. She was staying in the house. She cornered me and told me a long story—the day after I met Miss Benedet."

"What an infamous old woman!"

"She called herself a friend of yours—warned me for your sake, she said, and because she has sons of her own."

"Oh! Has she daughters?"

"Two—staying in the house."

"I see. She told it brutally, I suppose?"

"Quite so."

"Worse than I did, Willy?"

William the Silent held his peace.

"You did not believe it? How much of it did you believe?"

"Mother," he said, "do you think a man can't see what a girl is?"

"But what do you know about girls?"

"Where is she?"

"What!"

"Where is Helen? The man from Lord's said he brought her out here last night."

"Did you not get her letter?" Mrs. Thorne evaded.

"Where shall I find her?"

"Willy, I am a perjured woman! I have been making mischief steadily for two days."

"You might as well go on, mater." Willy beamed gravely upon his mother's career of dissimulation.

"Don't, for pity's sake, be hopeful! She said she would not see you for worlds."

"Then she hasn't gone."

Willy took a quick survey of the premises. He had long gray eyes and a set mouth. He saw most things that he looked at, and when he aimed for a thing he usually got somewhere near the mark.

"She is not in the house," he decided; "she is not on the hill—remains the garden."

* * *

Mrs. Thorne stood alone, meditating on Miss Benedet's trust in her. She saw her husband, her stool of repentance and her mercy-seat in one, plodding toward her contentedly across the soft garden ground, stepping between the lettuces and avoiding the parsley bed. He knocked off a huge fat kitchen weed with his cane.

"Where is that girl?" he said. "It's time you got your things on. We ought to be starting in ten minutes."

"If you can find Willy you'll probably find 'that girl'!" Mrs. Thorne explained, and then proceeded to explain further, as she walked with her husband back to the house.

"Well," he summed up, "what is your opinion of the universe up to date? Got any faith in anything left?"

WHAT IS ART FICTION?

The intersection of art and life. Painting with words. Portmay Press brings contemporary and classic works of art fiction to a wide readership.

OTHER TITLES OF INTEREST FROM PORTMAY PRESS

Art Fiction: Stories
Edited by Genevieve Sheets

Art Fiction Stories II
Edited by Ellen Francese

Marriage of the Smila-Hoffmans
Maryann D'Agincourt

To Let
John Galsworthy

The Professor's House
Willa Cather

Washington Square
Henry James

www.ingramcontent.com/pod-product-compliance
Lightning Source LLC
LaVergne TN
LVHW091011080826
845145LV00003B/1220

* 9 7 8 1 9 5 9 9 8 6 2 6 3 *